John Harris Knowles

To England and Back

A Winter Vacation

John Harris Knowles

To England and Back
A Winter Vacation

ISBN/EAN: 9783337251512

Printed in Europe, USA, Canada, Australia, Japan

Cover: Foto ©Andreas Hilbeck / pixelio.de

More available books at **www.hansebooks.com**

Miss M. G. Knowles,
from
J. H. Knowles,
Albany, Nov. 16, 1907,

TO
ENGLAND AND BACK

TO
ENGLAND AND BACK

A WINTER VACATION

BY

CANON KNOWLES

" Going, staying; staying, going,
Little recks the ready mind;
Wheresoe'er good work is doing
Richest realm he there shall find."

Goethe

CHICAGO
A. C. McCLURG AND COMPANY
1892

DEDICATION.

TO MY
MANY SYMPATHETIC FRIENDS AT HOME AND ABROAD,
WHO FOLLOWED MY
" WINTER VACATION " IN THE COLUMNS OF
" THE LIVING CHURCH,"
I DEDICATE THIS VOLUME, TRUSTING THAT THE LETTERS.
HERE PRESENTED IN MORE PERMANENT FORM,
MAY FIND WITH THEM A
RENEWED WELCOME AND AN ABIDING INTEREST,

J. H. K.

CONTENTS.

Contents.

XI.

XII.

XIII.

XIV.

XV.

XVI.

Contents.

TO ENGLAND AND BACK:

A

WINTER VACATION.

I.

THE rain and the loneliness at Twenty-second Street station, as we waited for the Lake Shore train to take us off east from Chicago on December 3d, exactly coincided with our feelings. Adieus had been all said, the past, like a great prairie, stretched out behind us, and it was just as well to be with one's own thoughts alone, as one looked out over such a vista of years. The lamps of Chicago seemed interminable; they lit up the scene, even as the lights of memory lit up the past.

A night's ride brought us to Cleveland, where we stayed over until Sunday afternoon, the guest of the Rev. T. C. Foote,

who has charge of St. James' church in
that city.   On Saturday we called on dear
Dr. Bolles, who received us with a loving
kiss and gave us his patriarchal blessing
as we left his venerable presence.   What
Church memories crowd up as one con-
verses with such a man: Crosswell, De
Lancey, the elder Doane, the Advent,
Boston, choral services, free churches, the
pioneer struggles for Church principles
for over fifty years past.   We saw some
of the fruits of such labor in St. James'
church, where we ministered next day.
An early Celebration at which we officiated was a refreshment to our souls, and
the children's Eucharist fully choral at
9:30, at which the rector, Rev. T. C.
Foote, celebrated, was beautiful in its
teaching power and reverent rendering.

Monday morning found us in New
York, the guest of Dr. Houghton, at the
Transfiguration.   What a haven of rest
is this secluded but ever-busy nook in the
turmoil of New York life!   After Matins
we went for steamer tickets and letter of
credit to Wall Street, and, in turning into
Trinity, as our custom is, we found a lecture, the first of a week's course, an-

nounced to be given at noon by Dr. Holland of St. Louis. The rain had followed us from Chicago, but it did not deter a goodly number from attending the lecture. Sharp on the stroke of twelve Dr. Holland entered the pulpit, while a few chorister boys in cassocks, one of the assistants of Trinity and Bishop Potter took their places in the stalls, a hymn was sung, and then, after a few collects and the Lord's Prayer, Dr. Holland began a discourse of marked brilliancy, lasting close on the hour; a collect or two at the close, and the blessing by the Bishop, concluded the service. There was a delicious freshness in the Doctor's manner, and a certain freedom of illustration, coupled with keen metaphysical insight, which aroused and retained attention all through.

Night found us at the seminary, renewing old memories and interweaving the past with the present, in the study of Prof. Richey, whom we found well and happy, and promising us before long a new volume of his valuable work on the parables of our Lord.

New York was in all its glory, winter though it was; so, the next day, under

bright skies, we took in the inimitable
beauty of Fifth Avenue from Twenty-
third Street to the Park. It is extensive
enough to have a vista like a mountain
gorge; whichever way you look it has
a charm and a character all its own. It
finds a fitting close in Central Park, where
lace-like, bare trees, dark pines and green
grass made a picture of rare beauty. No
wonder New Yorkers love New York.

In my many calls that day, perhaps in
a Churchly way the most interesting thing
to record was a magnificent pyx for taking the sacrament to the sick, which a
clergyman showed me. It was solid gold,
over two inches in circumference, set with
emeralds, pearls and diamonds, of real
beauty and excellent taste, and at a low
estimation, was valued at four thousand
five hundred dollars.

Wednesday, December 9th, found us at
10:30 A. M., on the steamship "Germanic,"
ready for the big ferry across the Atlantic,
but before that hour we had the loving
comfort of Celebration, receiving from
the hand of Father Prescott at the Transfiguration; we had Matins and Litany, at
which Dr. Houghton officiated, and had

his loving farewell as we left his door for the steamer.

Soon the time for all to go ashore came around, a few loving friends lingered to say to us a last adieu; out into the stream we pushed, and then out to sea.

"Germanic," December, 1891.

II.

FROM my experience in the "Germanic," in this month of December, 1891, I should certainly argue that winter is the best time to cross the Atlantic. We have had smooth seas, bright skies, clear weather, a cheerful, happy company, and no crowding. All these are advantages which I found absent on summer trips. Of course, we have had some severe rolls of the vessel and some seasickness, and a little discomfort to some passengers, but "I have not lost a meal," seasickness has not come near me. I have a psychical formula for its cure, which is this: Cultivate the Unconscious Automatic Equilibrium. Where put in practice, it never fails of effect. It is based upon the truth that we only know that which we are unconscious of knowing, and so when equilibrium becomes unconsciously automatic, we have our sea legs and are seasick proof. The mental effort to commit

the formula to memory is the first step in
the cure.   It diverts attention from inter-
nal disturbances and then the braced-up
being can begin unimpeded the Cultiva-
tion of the Unconscious Automatic Equilibrium.   It may be as well to add to this
a practical hint, to keep the knee and
ankle joints perfectly limber, to realize
that the horizon of the ocean is immov-
able as solid earth, and to consider motion
in all objects but one's self, the normal
condition of environment in the ship.   I
have given this valuable formula to fellow-
passengers, especially ladies, with never-
failing effect.   With two factors of stead-
iness established—one's own well balanced
brain and viscera, and the unswerving
circle of the sea—then the incidental motion of the ship will be soon as little re-
garded as the motion of a good horse or the
jolting of a carriage.   The heaving deck
will become a positive source of pleasure,
and will lose all its fearful terrors.

Our company in the saloon, in its
chance gathering of units into the brief
whole of an Atlantic voyage, had its
never-failing interest.   There were old
travelers who had encircled the globe

again and again; there were farmers from
Manitoba and Oregon homeward bound
once more for Christmas; there was the
silent old lady, with a sorrow at her heart,
which rumor told us was the dead body
of her daughter, also on board, on its
silent journey from Colorado to an English churchyard; there were Americans,
bound for the South of France for needed
rest, and so on and on. After some days
out, an old gentleman spoke to me; he
was from a town in Illinois, near Chicago,
and knew the C—s and the D—s and Mr.
S—, and Church life in Illinois for forty-
five years past. The first man I met on
board was from Chicago, and so, ere long,
we were all like a big family.

But oh, how lovely the sea was! One
evening it was all slate color and purple,
with yellow lights on the waves, caught
from the pale sunset. One night it was
steel-blue, plumed with silver-feathered
waves, dancing in the bright moonlight.
In the sky were soft masses of bright
white clouds, with great star lit spaces of
clear, open sky. It was a glory to walk
the deck on such a night.

One need never weary at sea, if there

is an eye for color and a heart for beauty.
If nothing else, there is the encircling
perfect curve of the horizon; but, through
this mystic circle the dolphins play and
the whales send up their spray and graceful gulls float about us. It is all color,
motion, never ceasing variety.

Sailors consider it a lucky omen to
have one parson on board; more than
this, it is said, brings bad luck, so it was
my fortune to be all alone in this capacity
and to take the services on Sunday.

We had our reverent worship in the
saloon, with the old familiar English
Prayer Book and Hymns Ancient and
Modern. A young lady from Manitoba,
played the hymns and all joined heartily
in their singing. There is something
always touching in the sound of human
voices on the sea, as they are lifted in the
songs of home or of heaven. Our hymns
had the pathos which ever pertains to
such conditions. I shall not soon forget
our congregation of that day; close by
was a leading actress from a London
theatre with some of her people devoutly
joining; in front was my old friend from
near Chicago, though I did not know

then who he was; not far off was a young mother from far northwestern Canada, with her little boy, a dream of beauty and as good as gold. She told me that she had traveled fifty miles to have him baptized "in church," as she said with proper emphasis.

Although a sermon is not usually expected or encouraged at sea, yet I ventured a few words, taking as my theme the verse of the psalm, "They that go down to the sea in ships," etc. My theme was the sea a revealer of God, and the ship a teacher of human duty to God and to our neighbor. The sea revealed God — in its infinity — as being the source of life — as being changeless under apparent change. The ship taught liberty of will within prescribed limits; obedience to constituted authority and the united interest of all humanity. Brevity had to be studied. After the service the purser said it was all right and so all were pleased. In another Sunday we shall all be scattered, never perhaps to meet again; soon land will be reached and our voyage will come to an end.

At Sea, December 15, 1891.

III.

MY first Sunday in the old land was bright and beautiful, not a breath of air stirring and a delicious tender sky with fleecy clouds hung over all. It was hard to think the balmy air was in December weather. A brisk walk from Black-rock brought us through part of Cork to the splendid cathedral of St. Finn Bar. This is a graceful structure with three massive stone spires. It is from a design by Burgess and is more Norman than Gothic in appearance, having a decidedly foreign air, unlike the English ideal. One of the chief charms of the interior is that from no point can you see the entire extent. There is always something unseen and beyond.

The service happened to be an ordination. There were two candidates for the diaconate and four for the priesthood. Matins were sung with full choir and with good effect. The boys' voices were well trained in a soft, delicate manner, and the general effect was tender and sympathetic, but all was taken in such a high pitch and with such rapidity that congregational participation was out of the question. One or two conscientious individuals near me were doing their best to join in, utterly unconscious of the ludicrous effect of a man full grown, singing off the Confession in a high falsetto manner. All around was silence except from those few absurd attempts to make the people's part a reality with vocal expression. A low pitch for Confession and all the opening part of the service, with the plain song in unison by choir and people, would make all right and vastly popularize the choral service.

Matins over a fine sermon was preached by Dean Warren, on the text, "Sanctify them through Thy truth." Its aim was to show the importance of a consecrated ministry and its work in this present world. It led up to the sacramental idea, but did not express it or even allude to it.

The alms of the people were at this point collected and offered, and thereupon, until the close of the service, the people kept dribbling out of the church. First, the choir left in a body, and then without note of music or any adjunct whatever, suggesting the greater solemnities, the services of ordination and the Holy Eucharist were proceeded with.

After the eloquent sermon by the Dean and the emphasis he put upon the ministry and its work, it seemed a strange thing to put the conferring of such a dignity and the exercise of its greatest power in such a corner.

The dribble of the congregation went on and on until at the close about fourteen people remained in the church outside of the clergy. It was hopeful to hear the clear Catholic ring of the Ordinal, which fortunately (providentially, rather, one should write) has received none of the damaging changes sustained by other portions of the Prayer Book of the Church of Ireland.

A young Irish friend with me heard with astonishment the words: "Whose sins thou dost forgive, they are forgiven, and whose sins thou dost retain, they are retained." He had never seen an ordination before, he had heard the priest-

hood denied, he did not know such words
were in the book, he never knew that the
priesthood in the church of Ireland was
thus asserted and as clearly conveyed. To
judge of the effect upon my young friend,
it seemed a pity that such a teaching rite
was administered in an emptied church.

The afternoon was spent in lovely
walks through woods and fields, watching
the pearly tints of the setting sun. A
landscape, beautiful as Italy, stretched
before us, tall pines rising above the elms
and beeches suggested the summer land;
neither was the sentiment arising from
the decay of ancient splendor absent, for
we had our walk through the unoccupied
park of a vast deserted mansion. We
had rambled through its halls and corridors, climbed its marble staircase, entered
the great silent ballroom, and traversed
the tumble-down conservatory, where a
passion flower still trailed its pathetic ten-
drils, and a Virginia creeper was even yet
bravely in bloom. How sad it all was,
yet the view from the windows over the
Lee was like Tivoli, the mirth and grace
of human life had all passed away. What
will the new order bring?

The new order in the Church promises something at least; neatness, order, interest, all indicate progress. At the cathedral the Dean gave out notice of a first Celebration at seven, Christmas morning, a second Celebration, choral, at eight, and choral Matins and sermon by the Lord Bishop at 11:30 A. M. I wish I could be present, but I must be among my own kindred in the rural parish where they dwell, where also are the graves of a household.

At night we worshipped in the church at Blackrock. The singing was quite fair from a choir of men and women, the congregation though thin, was devout, and the sermon, if not eloquent, was earnest and helpful. The stars lit us home through the windings of the way which here and there resounded with songs whose refrains reminded us that we were within the range of that inexplicable relation, Irish politics.

Golden Terrace, Blackrock,
   December 27, 1891.

IV.

PERHAPS you would like to know how I spent my Christmas Day in Ireland. Come with me, then, as we drive through eight miles of water-soaked country under a cloudy sky to Kilmallock. Do not suppose, however, that the drive is unpleasant. Far from it. The fields are green, the air is mild, cattle are in the pastures, and the occasional song of a bird is heard.

The winding road brings us at last in sight of the town. It lies among meadows through which flows in graceful curves, a river whose poetical Celtic name is Lubach or The Dawn. Within the embrace of this flood stands an ancient ruin, once the happy home of Dominicans. The Irish Archæological Society has recently put it in some order, and the graceful lancet windows and unroofed nave, aisles, choir, and great square tower look interesting and picturesque. Not far

off is one of the ancient gates of the
town, under which, in days of old, many
an armed band entered with booty or
passed forth to war. It is now in better
use, being occupied by a school. Within
the town is another ruin, the ancient
church of SS. Peter and Paul. It has
nave and aisles and chapels, and one of
Ireland's famous round towers; all open
to the sky, and embowered in luxurious
ivy. The choir of this ancient church is
roofed in and fitted for divine service.
The sweet-toned bell was ringing out
from the round tower, still used as a
belfry, as we entered. We found the
services fairly rendered. The hymns were
the familiar *Adeste Fideles* and " Hark,
the herald angels sing." The chants of
Matins were also sung, the choir, consisting of ladies and gentlemen, giving them
with great sweetness. But here too, as
elsewhere in Ireland, not a note of music
was used in the celebration, and the same
sad exodus took place, eight or ten remained for the Holy Eucharist, all the
rest departed. We noticed that in the
Irish Prayer Book the eastward position
is prohibited, and the clergyman is for-

bidden, while offering prayer, to turn his back upon the people. The effect of this in the conduct of the service, seems strangely irreverent to one accustomed to our American ways. Crosses over the altar, or anywhere in the church, we found also explicitly prohibited. How strange! in the Church of St. Patrick, and in a land whose most dignified monuments are the existing crosses of the ancient Irish Church!

We had in the service an excellent sermon, delivered without manuscript, from the rector. His red hood declared him to be a D. D. from Trinity College, Dublin. It was from the text: "What think ye of Christ?" It was an appeal for fullness of knowledge as to the veritable Manhood and Godhead of our Blessed Lord. It lacked the practical application which might be given, by pointing out how access to that Manhood and to that Godhead might now be had through the Blessed Sacraments; but it may seem ungracious thus to criticise. Perhaps the art of the sermon was in permitting the hearer to make this application, silently, for himself.

The ancient choir thus fitted up for worship presented a plain appearance. There was some Christmas decoration of the traditional holly and ivy, and a holly wreath, suggesting by its very circle, a traversing cross, hung over the Holy Table. The most beautiful thing in the church was the graceful five-lancet window in the east end, a relic of past ages. The whole place was devoid of ornament, except the mural tablets to departed social greatness, but this five-light lancet window shed over all a tone of solemnity and distinction.

As we left the church, groups of eager-looking lads and lasses lined the way at each side, evidently expecting something. What this was, we soon learned when we saw the rector scattering coppers among them for an indiscriminate scramble. There was fun and shouting from the merry group, during which we mounted our trap and drove home to a happy fireside and pleasant cheer, having on the whole a very happy Christmas Day in Ireland.

Adamstown, Knocklong,
December 30, 1891.

V.

MY little visit to Dublin had some
points of Church interest. My
Sunday was spent there, and coincided
with the general excitement caused by
the lamented death of Prince Albert Victor, Duke of Clarence and Avondale. I
went to St. Bartholomew's at eleven
o'clock, and found a most refreshing
service. The church is beautiful, a gothic
structure well put together, with a peculiar arrangement of the transepts, each of
which is composed of two bays, placed
side by side, with supporting pillars
between the two. This gives space and
variety, and does away with the necessity
of the expensive construction of roof
where the transepts are built as high as
the nave. By the church is a commodious
church hall, and yet again near that, a
fair vicarage; church and all enclosed in
one garden.

The chancel was well furnished, need-

ing only the lights; the service was fully
choral, Matins and Celebration; the boys'
voices were of surpassing sweetness, and
the music was reverently done; care was
shown in every detail, the Gregorian
chanting of the Psalter being as tenderly
done as the most elaborate part of the
service. How good it was to be one of
such a worshipping congregation! There
seemed to be no fear of external reverence, and one could see here and there
the use of the sacred sign. We had a sermon on the Marriage in Cana of Galilee,
a clear, out-spoken Catholic sermon, with
no uncertain sound. I must mention a
point the preacher made which occurred
to myself when studying the miracle. It
was this, that there is no reason why we
should conclude that all the water in the
waterpots was turned into wine. The
letter would imply that only the water
which was drawn out was thus miracu-
lously changed. I remember seeing a
picture once where this idea was depicted
as the water from one of the vessels was
being poured into that in the hands of
the servant, the curving stream in the
descent showed the change from the

clear water to the ruddy wine. The reverent awe on the faces of the servants gave comment to the wonder.

As I followed the service, I saw how impossible it is by repressive rubric to hinder the outcome of truth. The preacher was also Celebrant, and even if he had not referred in his sermon to the Real Presence, one would have known his faith to see him at the altar. It was indeed a delight to be at St. Bartholomew's, Dublin.

In the afternoon we went to St. Patrick's. How pathetic it is to enter such a place. The traditions of Church and State still linger there. The banners of the knights hang down over the stalls in the choir with the helmets and swords of chivalry, but how different all was from the tone at St. Bartholomew's!

The choir had about it all, a sort of sturdy, honest irreligiousness. They came in, eyes all about them. They took their places and lolled about bravely. They sang well and lustily. That *they* should sing was evidently the reason, and the prime reason, of their being there. So it went.

The organ was gloriously played by
Sir Robert Stewart, sympathetic to the
last degree. His improvisation at the
commencement of service was masterly;
at first a few notes; then a gradual in-
crease until the majestic organ throbbed
with life under his facile hands. All
round him through the service were
young men who hung upon his every
action, and helped him *con amore* with
the stops. Beautiful it was, like a father
with his children, but there was danger
in it too, for at times, proceedings which
might not be really so, looked like indif-
ference or irreverence. What musician
is there that does not know the dangers
which lurk about an organ keyboard during divine service.

The Psalms were splendidly chanted
to florid chants: such a contrast to the use
of St. Bartholomew, where the psalter
stood out in most impressive simplicity.
One does not care particularly for the
words in such rapturous harmonies, but
in the simple style, the words are everything. The service was Stewart, full of
melody, one anthem was by Spohr, and
the second the grand old composition by

Blow, " I beheld, and lo, a great multitude." I had not heard it for many and
many a year, but fresh and vivid and picturesque it was as ever. The tenor solo,
" These are they," was especially touching. I fear it might be considered tedious nowadays, I mean the anthem as a
whole. For American use, some of its
involved verse parts might be cut out.
Enough is left of simple grandeur and
effective music to make a most impressive
addition to choir music.

The whole service was a grand one.
The crowded church, the aged and venerable clergy, and the eloquent sermon
with loyal allusion in pathetic phrases to
the great sorrow known to all, made a
magnificent whole. It was too dark and
too late to visit the tomb of Swift and the
well of St. Patrick, which still bubbles
up within the church. Indeed, it was
hard to move out of the building, for the
great congregation at the close of service surged up into the choir to pass by
the organ and organist as the Dead
March, from Saul, gave forth its solemn
strains.

Through the crowded streets we walked to the Shelbourne, where the evening was spent in pleasant converse about Chicago friends and others. It came about this way: I noticed at the *table d'hote* a gentleman whom I thought must be an American. He had a certain quick way about him, alert and keen. He nervously wiped his plate off once with his napkin. He seemed to be wide awake all over, he took the little bit of ice cream they give you on this side, in a bite or two, and asked for more; so, at the first opportunity, I bowed to him, feeling he must be an American. I was mistaken. When I entered the reading room after dinner on Sunday night, he bowed to me, opened a conversation at once, and when he heard of Chicago, he surprised me further by saying: " I heard a grand sermon on Atheism once, from your Bishop out there, when he was visiting Bermuda, where I was stationed with my regiment." So there was, after all, a link between us.

What a talk we had there. I hope I talked " wiser than I knew," for in that

little group by the fire in the Dublin inn,
were gone over all manner of questions
relating to American affairs, religious,
social, political, and prospective.

Dublin, January 18, 1892.

VI.

AFTER leaving Dublin, my next point was near Newry, at the hospitable home of my friend, the rector of Donaghmore. Years had elapsed since we walked together as friends in Chicago, but bright and fresh was the cheery voice which greeted us on the railway platform at Goraghwood, where we got off our train.

The snow lingered here and there, as we drove four miles over hill and dale to our destination, the way enlivened by many a question of places and friends at the other side. How lovely are such meetings of friends; tinged they must be with a certain tone of sadness, for years have flown, and changes have come, and friends are spoken of who cannot answer ever here on earth again: *Adsum!*

The Rev. Mr. Cowan showed us the grey outside of his church, with its tall square tower in the dim light of evening, and soon thereafter we were within the warm walls of the rectory, and could enjoy the clamor of the crows outside in the swaying tree tops. Our good friend was a little solicitous about our comfort in our room, and suggested for us a fire, " but," said he, " I shall have to get a crow's nest dug out of the chimney first." Well, of course I could not be so selfish as to permit such an interesting domestic establishment to be uprooted for my luxury, so I did without the fire, and learned the knack of avoiding the sharp chill of linen sheets by sleeping boldly next the blankets. In the morning I felt no ill from the cold room—rather the reverse— helped too by the consciousness of not having dealt any cruelty to animals.

I found Donaghmore church and graveyard a most interesting study. The church is on the site of an ancient foundation of the Culdees, and the site itself, as well as some of the surrounding fields, contains many curious and extensive subterranean constructions. These interesting remains of either a warlike or ascetic use, were accidentally discovered in low-

ering the level of the road bed near the
graveyard. At the same time portions of
an ancient Celtic cross were also un-
earthed, and through the pious care of
the rector, aided by the enlightened and
unprejudiced spirit of the parishioners,
were reverently re-erected on their ancient site close by the church. It was
found that the main entrance to those
underground passages and retreats was
at the foot of the ancient cross. Here an
opening was left, but strange to say, had
to be closed up again, because of the
offensive odors coming forth. Think of
it, for over eight hundred years the
stratum of earth above the excavation
has been used for purposes of burial,
hence the doleful foulness which finds
escape into those hollow chambers of
the past. Perhaps when our civiliza-
tion has attained a period of three thousand years, and we are face to face in
many places with those conditions of
mortality, then cremation may not seem
so dreadful or unnatural. Direct earth
burial and displacement of bones after a
certain number of years, as is the manner

in France and other countries, seems an improvement on the reeking graveyards to be met with in these old lands.

A few peaceful days passed too swiftly under the rectory roof. There were rides over the country, beautiful at all times. There was a lovely day at Dromantine, amid the glories of the pleasure grounds, even in winter a thing of beauty, the arboretum, the pinetum, the greenhouses, the old gardener, the older oaks and beeches, each grey and grizzled by many a winter, and then there was the splendid home, the ample cheer, and the hearty welcome.

From Donaghmore I turned my steps to Belfast, whither I went with my good host, and had the privilege of attending a meeting of the clergy of the united dioceses of Down, Connor, and Dromore, convened for the purpose of passing resolutions of condolence and respect, in connection with the death of Prince Albert Victor. It was a splendid body of clergy, there are over two hundred in the united dioceses. It was beautiful to see the love and loyalty which found expression in every face, and in every word uttered.

As I listened I thought of the wolf hound which art ever depicts *couchant* by the Irish harp. No harsh treatment can blunt the sense of truthful affection in such a noble creature, and so from the Irish Church, despoiled and betrayed as it has been, there ever comes the unquenchable spirit of heartfelt loyalty. It was good to be there. Barring the purpose of the meeting I could almost fancy myself at a deanery meeting at home on an extended scale, and I thought too I could see parallels to some of my dear remembered friends. More than one good brother invited me to stay over and preach, but I was bound to be in London on the twenty-fourth, and to bring that about with ease I had to leave Greenore for Holyhead on Friday night. Of that journey I remember the gloomy turn-out at two in the morning at Holyhead, and the dreary wait in black Holyhead station until six. The fancy came to me in the stuffy damp atmosphere, that the air of England was breathed over and over too much, its very vitality exhausted, but possibly we make our own atmosphere, and my jaded condition made me a bad judge. At last the train was made up, and in four or five hours we were whirled through a rain-sodden country into the heart of London.

On the way there was much to see, but the best of all things were the English themselves. What matters it, said I, should England cease to be an agricultural country, if she will only produce Englishmen, she will bring forth one of the noblest products of the earth.

London, January 22, 1892.

VII.

I HAVE been to the Abbey this morning, wandering down there leisurely, in time for 10 o'clock Matins. The sun, like a great ball of glistening copper, shone a distinct sphere through the dim atmosphere, and a rimy frost was under foot. On and on, by Westminster Bridge, by St. Margaret's, and into the Abbey by the restored transept entrance, with the beautiful new statue of the Holy Mother and her Divine Child adorning the same; one thinks of Laud and St. Mary's, Oxford, as one enters.

The Abbey is always impressive, the aspiring columns, the embowered roof, the luxuriant reverence of the fretted windows, lift one above the fretful impudence of the many monuments which too often encumber the glorious Minster. But we pass them all by now, and await in the choir the coming service. The stalls are all alight with candles protected by glass shades from the many draughts. Away on high, as one looks down the nave, glints of gold break in from outside, while all else in the venerated space is lost in gloom; a few people are present, strangers, like myself, and others who, evidently, are constant comers. At last the silence is broken by a chanted Amen, the organ wakes up to its harmony, the verger draws aside the curtains at the choir entrance, and choristers, precentor, canons, and dean, all take their places. There is no attempt at display or form, a little more of which might take away from the straggling appearance of big boys and little boys, long surplices and short surplices, all placed and put on without any apparent thought of order or beauty.

The service was sung to music of the old English school, contrapuntal, unsympathetic, and cold; perhaps from this very reason more suitable to a choir of unimpassioned voices. The mechanical ictus of a musical figure is more capable of being well taken by an average boy, than any tender stress or expression which emotion and good taste must understand

and seize. I can readily believe that such rebounding mechanical music could be as interesting to a boy as a game of hand ball or cricket. It hardly suits, however, the requirements of the heart. All was, of course, beautiful, and the voices harmonious, with a kind of prim prettiness in the sweet tones of the responces floating under the lofty and time-worn arches. One's thoughts stretched back to other occupants of that choir, whose throats were lusty and strong with the sturdy song of Gregory, and whose members filled up every stall. Now we have dean and canons few, and a little double ribband of choristers filling in with white a few feet at each side in the splendid length of that matchless choir.

The first Lesson was read by Canon Farrar. It was the pathetic story of Joseph sold by his brethren, and the " vesture dipped in blood " brought to the heart-broken Jacob. A touch of genuine pathos rang through the simple, dignified reading, and I was near enough to see a dimness in the eye as he uttered the words, " My son is not." It was beautiful.

The second Lesson was read by the

dean. It was the account of our Lord walking upon the water, and St. Peter's heroic desire to come to Him thereon. The tone was different, and the unconscious art not so effective as in Canon Farrar's reading, but both Lessons were the living effective part of the service from an emotional aspect.

The anthem was a commonplace affair by Rogers, I think, nothing but a succession of sounds on the words: "Ye that by night stand in the house of the Lord." Not quite the thing for Matins. Ah, if the pathos of first or second Lesson had been taken up in the anthem and emphasized by the glory of good music, and that good choir, how well it would have been! It might have been the sorrow of Jacob, or the aspiring faith of Peter, or the assuring voice of Christ, but instead it was a selection without thought.

The service over, I went once round the Abbey and the chapels clustered about the incomparable chapel of Henry the Seventh. What thoughts come as one goes from the shrine of the Confessor to that tomb of another Edward, which declares the stripling to be "Under

Christ, Head of the Church of England."
It is all a pathetic jumble of fearful
events. Elizabeth and Mary sleep side by
side. Mary Stuart rests beyond. Here
altars are torn away, and tombs of cour-
tiers and kings, favorite ladies and war-
riors, take the place of the saints. Watt,
of steam-engine fame, in colossal marble,
speaks of the new age amid the crumbling monuments of ancient faith. Mrs.
Siddons, in the grand air of a stage
queen, stands where the altar stood in St.
Michael's chapel. What a change! So
it is on every hand. Above are the glorious arches which looked down on the
ages of faith, around are the ashes of the
holy dead, but encrusted over all is the
pride and pomp of civil and political life.
William Pitt dominates in marble the
great entrance, while Fox continues ever
dying near by, in colossal effigy. It is all
a glorious pantheon of England's material
greatness and achievement in controversy,
statesmanship, war, research, letters, and
arts. It makes the heart throb and the
blood to tingle to wander under the sacred
arches of Westminster, whether one
thinks of the past or the present.

In a little enclosed space to the right of the main entrance, stands a monument and bust of Keble. It is a gem in design, of jewelled marbles, enclosing the sweet face of the poet of the "Christian Year." Opposite are busts of Kingsley and Frederick Denison Maurice, but these are placed, not looking out to the altar, as Keble does, but looking the other way. I could not but fancy that the soul of Keble was thus looking out over the Abbey and the English Church, and waiting and hoping for better things. With slow steps I wandered on, over the graves of mighty men, out into the crowded thoroughfare, on by Downing street and the Horse Guards, by White-hall and Trafalgar Square, by Pall Mall and Regent street, until I found myself in the church of St. Thomas, where, in the silence of the sanctuary and the in-cense-laden atmosphere, I had a good pray and a good rest, in the stillness, after my week-day morning in the Abbey.

London, January 23, 1892.

VIII.

WHEN one has only a few Sundays in London, it is extremely difficult to choose just where to go. Well, on this occasion I gave myself dispensation, and went on my first Sunday to the Brompton Oratory, to see what it was like; so soon too after Manning's death a certain feeling impelled me that possibly there might have been some allusion to him. There was none, however.

The Oratory is a beautiful structure in the style of St. Paul's, smaller, but much more ornate, gold and glitter is on every hand. At every convenient place in the graceful structure there is an altar, and each altar is fully decorated; every corner is utilized, even the dark space under the gallery, which holds the choir and organ, is turned into a gloomy Calvary, with the sacred Sufferer in a position of intense agony, the thieves in contortions on either side, and Mary and St. John at either hand. The high altar has a grand effect, with a suspended baldachino simulating in metal a rich tapestry. The use of so much gorgeous marble and gilt ornamentation might be called overdone, at least to our taste. Punctually at the stroke of eleven, the officiants entered, and the organ began. The whole service was marked by the most careful and graceful attention to detail, the vestments were never awry, all was spick and span, clean and neat, and well done. Italian it was in spirit and form, but it was done by Englishmen, and done perfectly. The acolytes were men and well trained, while priest, deacon, and sub-deacon showed in every movement, thought, reverence, and dignity. It was an object lesson in propriety, surely it was not out of place to be thus careful and absorbed in the worship of God. My mind reverted to much elsewhere that was ever the reverse, where individual whim and untutored awkwardness marred obvious propriety. I was especially touched with the entire naturalness and fitness of the Kiss of Peace, given and received before the Communion of the priest. I wonder such an ancient, beautiful, and fitting symbolism has not been restored, as it easily might, to our own use.

The music was exquisitely rendered. The choir of men and boys occupy a gallery well down in the nave, and are not seen. Hence all the necessary direction of a conductor can be used without distraction or any unedifying effect. I could see from where I sat, the incessant action which he kept over the music, minutely guiding every phrase. From this cause the Gregorian numbers were given with a tender delicacy and careful expression, quite surprising, and the more elaborate figured music of the Mass was rendered with positive passion. A grand adult voice sang an offertory from Gounod.

The sermon was a plain, straight-forward, teaching sermon upon Confession, based upon the words of the Gospel, " Lord, if Thou wilt, Thou canst make me clean." The church was quite well filled, and the congregation seemed decidedly English. The Italian mission, as Archbishop Benson calls the Roman Church in England, is but a small thing compared to the great Church of the land. I felt this as I stood a few hours later under the dome of St. Paul's, and heard and saw that vast congregation heartily joining and intelligently joining, in the psalms, and prayers, and hymns. I felt too, that, as one day is with the Lord as a thousand years, and a thousand years as one day, so in His good Providence there may be work for both Churches to do for each other, until that time shall come "that they all may be one." There is a vast movement going on among all Christians, which is filled with a purpose we may not dare to limit, or to measure. "Yes," I heard a gentleman of a clerical cut say to another of like appearance, one week-day in St. Paul's, "a great revolution in opinion and practice is passing over the Presbyterians in England and Scotland." "Yes," said the other, "we find the same in America." They were two Presbyterian ministers comparing notes under the dome of St. Paul's, and before the reredos, with the carven Christ, His Blessed Mother, and the saints thereon. "That they may be one!"

Canon Scott Holland was the preacher.

It was a delight to watch his intent, clear face, and listen to his impassioned, grandly delivered sermon. Of every service at St. Paul's one can only repeat phrases of praise. This was as all the rest, splendid.

London, January 24, 1892.

IX.

IT was my good fortune to be present at the patronal festival of St. Paul's cathedral. At ten o'clock we had Matins and High Celebration, Canon Scott Holland being Celebrant. It was a glorious function. The service was sung by the ordinary choir, augmented in the Communion service by a full orchestra. The Mass was Weber in E flat. I was somewhat curious to hear such music, thus rendered. The general impression was good, the orchestra giving life and expression to the boys' voices. In all the massive choral effects, it was most devotional; but such music illustrates the extreme difficulty of reaching that *very little* which constitutes perfection, or the tolerated approach thereto. I wish I could remember what Browning says on this matter, but I am away from books, and cannot call it to mind. Those who know will remember, and those who do not know will never mind.

When Matins were over, I wish you could experience the effect of the sudden burst of orchestral music from the hidden instrumentalists, as they played the prelude to the Introit, Baden Powell's "Hail, Festal Day." It gave me a choking sensation of happiness and inspiration. The service, Weber in E flat, adapted to Anglican use, and omitting *Benedictus* and *Agnus Dei*, was then sung. One must confess that in the fugal work, and in the solo soprano parts, there was some weakness, but this arose more from the character of the music, which was never written for boys' voices, than from any want of skill in the choristers. The wonder is they did so well, without the guidance of a baton and the prompting of a conductor. A *Salutaris Hostia*, by Gounod, was sung after Consecration, in English of course, and was most inspiring. Why, I could not help asking, should such difficult music be sung while kneeling? It is an added strain upon the choristers, which is not required. The people kneel, but, according to ancient custom, the choir should stand at all times when singing, except in Requiems, at the *Agnus Dei*, and on a few special occasions of penitence. For the sake of the teaching, a hymn of adoration, to very simple music, might be sung kneeling, but to sing elaborate Mass music in *Sanctus, Benedictus*, and *Agnus Dei*, on one's knees, makes a difficult thing still more difficult, and needlessly so.

Taking the service as a whole, the most perfect vocalization was in the sevenfold Amen of Sir John Stainer, sung after Consecration and the Blessing. One might wish that he never should hear it anywhere else, except in St. Paul's, London, for it would seem that there only are its rapturous cadences to be heard in perfection.

I must add about the service, that the altar lights were lit, and that there was no pause after the prayer for Christ's Church Militant; no withdrawal of the people at that point; and that the vergers seemed to limit the number of communicants. This great service and grand congregation was but the prelude to the popular and splendid function at four o'clock, when Evensong and the larger portion of Mendelssohn's St. Paul was rendered by a body of four hundred voices and a full orchestra.

I had the good fortune to find a special nook of vantage near the choir, by the kindness of one of old St. Paul's boys whom I met, and so I could see the quiet way in which that large body of singers took their places, instrumentalists and all. These, arrayed, it must be confessed, in rather Falstaffian surplices, of bedgown shape and ancient hue, some of them, dropped into their places by twos and threes as they got ready; after them, the vast body of bass voices at one side, and the tenors at the other, then the boys from the Chapel Royal, Westminster, and elsewhere. All seated, the regular choir of St. Paul's and the clergy entered the stalls. There was no attempt at processional singing, and the quiet of the arrangement made amends for the omission, if such it was. When the officiating clergy reached their places, the whole vast congregation, filling the enormous spaces of St. Paul's, rose to their feet, all knelt for the moment of silent prayer,

and then, with this most impressive prelude, the service went on. The Psalms
were special, and sung by the regular
choir alone, all the voices in a thunderous
unison coming in with full organ and
orchestra on each *Gloria Patri*. Oh,
how glorious and thrilling it was! One
would listen to the tender harmonies of
the perfect chanting, and await with a
pleasure which was almost a pain, the
mighty crash of voices, organ and orchestra. All evidently did not feel the artistic
effect of this prepared contrast as I did,
for over the congregation could be heard
the *sotto voce* murmuring of the people
as they joined the choir while chanting
the familiar Psalms they had learned to
love. How much there is in this learn-
ing to love the Psalms, and this, in a
most marked way, is the privilege of the
Anglican Church. The *Magnificat* and
Nunc Dimittis were by Martin, in A.
The composer himself, the talented suc-
cessor of Sir John Stainer at the organ
of St. Paul's, conducted them and the
rest of the service from an estrade in the
centre, but concealed somewhat from the
people by the huge lectern. He was most

reverent and devout in his every act, and my heart quite went out to him as he knelt down for the versicles and prayers, conducting in that attitude with effect and dignity every cadence and amen.

But now the third collect is ended and the solemn music begins. All are seated, and the overture to St. Paul is rendered by the orchestra, then follows without break or pause, that portion of the oratorio from the conversion to the final chorus. I never heard before such singing of the duet, "Now we are ambassadors," or the air, "O God, have mercy," or the grand choruses, "How great is the depth," and all the others in that portion of the composition. There was not the slightest flavor of the concert room. It was religious, through and through, and every singer seemed to know the music as one does "Old Hundred." So there was a fervor, a subdued power which conscious power can alone give. No fuss, no strain, no effort, but reverent, good, honest, loving singing. I have heard our own societies sing in the Auditorium, and I am still proud of such a Chicago development, but it was artificial; I must even say

it sounded commonplace, when compared
to the effect of the music at this festival
at St. Paul's. The Auditorium, the
singers in evening dress, the varied cos-
tumes of the ladies, the orchestra *en evidence*, the people in their paid-for places,
the applause—how different from the
damp-stained walls of St. Paul's, the
lofty dome, the memories of centuries, the
vast body of all sorts and conditions of men
in the gloomy, half-lit spaces of the vast
cathedral, the constant reverent silence,
the great choir and orchestra in one mass
of white, the vested bishop and many dig-
nitaries, and the great altar of St. Paul's
—a dominating mystic presence over all,
with its lights aflame—made up a picture
and an effect not easily forgotten.

And all this in London, in the heart
of the world's trade, in the very court of
Mammon—all this, all this! I thought
and wondered if we shall ever have in
Chicago such a glorious structure as St.
Paul's, and such a gathering on the festival of the Conversion of the Apostle to
the Gentiles. Confident I am that such
a possibility would be the only fitting
crown of glory for the future London of

our mighty West, an assertion of spiritual reality arising out of and consecrating all material greatness.

I stood outside and watched the vast congregation melt away into the wonderful, ever more wonderful, London life. The soot-stained columns of St. Paul's looked grandly down, subliming the very filth of London; above were the clanging peals, more touching to me than Wagner's bells in " Parsifal," for they sounded not upon a mimic stage, but in the very heart of all modern life, telling of a Holy Grail which each must, if he would truly live, forever seek. St. Paul's words remain: "God forbid that I should glory save in the Cross of our Lord Jesus Christ, by which the world is crucified unto me, and I unto the world." What, if when one passes out of this great gathering and sees before his eyes again, want and vice, as see them he will, God has witness in all things, and the cross which dominates from the top of St. Paul's is symbol of the triumph which the Cross will surely bring—and so the Festival for me closes.

London, January 25, 1892.

X.

WHAT contrasts may come to one in London in the ordinary incidents of an unpremeditated stroll! After breakfast I went to the National Gallery and there feasted my eyes on one of the best collections of pictures in Europe. It is all free as air, and every picture plainly marked, so that all may understand as they go along. It would be tedious to detail this or that picture, and many of them are so well known by print and photograph, that it is like seeing an old friend in a magnificent new dress when one comes on the great original in this wonderful gallery. Why, one exclaims, there is Landseer's "High and Low Life," there is his "Dignity and Impudence," there is one of Constable's great landscapes, there is the Hobbema we have learned to love in etchings, there is Frith's "Derby Day," and there are Turner's glorious dreams of beauty and

mystery, the "Old Temeraire," and the
"Landing of the Prince of Orange," and
so with all the old friends of friends of
art, Etty, and Mulready, and Maclise and
others without number. But all this is
but a moiety of what is yet beyond and
beyond. Raphael's incomparable Madon-
nas, Botticelli's truthful and reverential
creations—there they all are, gleaming
welcome to our satiated eyes—Titian,
Francia, Orcagna, all royal names in art,
until we come to their worthy peer, Ros-
setti's Annunciation. What a pity it is
that one will get tired in a picture gallery, but tire you will, from the very
glory of the place, so one leaves with a
painful, weary sense of almost disrespect-
ful regard for all that is left behind unknown and unlooked at.

Go, one must, but ere I went I determined to give one look at least at the
Turner drawings. When I was last in
London, they were housed in a dark
basement, and half hidden in cabinets, but
now they have a bright lodgement in
many well-lighted rooms, and all are
framed upon the spacious walls, and well
they deserve it. If you ever, dear reader,

come to London, be sure you visit the
Turner drawings. There you see the
very soul of the man at work, and if you
have read Ruskin, you will understand
better than ever before his enthusiastic
criticisms of Turner. You will be fascin-
ated every moment of your stay. It may
be by the exquisite finish of sepia drawings for engravings, or the grand jotting
down of Alpine scenery with a few
blotches of color, and a minute touch here
and there of pen or pencil, or it may be
the perfect effect of complete transcrip-
tion accomplished with a simplicity that
absolutely dazzles.

After leaving the National Gallery, we
walked off to number thirty-two Little
Queen Street, the office of *The Church
Times.* Here we found sad affliction.
Only the day before, Mr. George J.
Palmer, the founder and proprietor of
that excellent church paper, had breathed
his last. We were received with great
kindness by his son, but after expressing
our most earnest sympathy we quickly
withdrew. With a sense of personal loss
we came out into the busy street, thinking of the many years the weekly visit of

The Church Times had been to us as the visit of a friend. On and on we went and soon found ourselves at Guildhall. The great hall itself where civic banquets are wont to be held, a grand gothic structure, gave us much to admire, while we watched the bewigged lawyers and their clients walking about. From this seething stream of life it was a pleasant change to visit the Free Library, and see the "pale clerks" bending over their books; and further on, to walk through the museum and see objects of continued interest; among others, a collection of impressions of the great seals of England from seven hundred and fifty-seven to the present date. From Guildhall another vague stroll brought us to London Bridge, over it, and back again. Leaning over the parapets one could watch the swift current of the receding tide, the flying barges, and the forest of shipping further on, or turning to the living torrent on the bridge, one might study its awful stream for hours. On every hand life is teeming. It is not merely the great throng upon the enormous bridge, but far beneath, at each side of the great approaches, other throngs have place. You look down into Lower Thames Street, and there another type of being seems to exist; fishermen and dock-hands, and stevedores, with warehouses and gin shops on every hand. In the midst of all this bustle and grime stood a church. What must it be to work in such a place; great the labor, and great the reward. Down I must go into the midst of the turmoil, and go I did. It seems almost wrong to be lounging round among such toilers, wrong to merely gaze at them, but if my attitude and face expressed what my heart felt, then my sympathy and respect for them would secure me respect also.

Great lines of men were toiling out from the ships over plank after plank, up ladders and on to wagons far down the street, each man with a box of oranges resting on his bent head and shoulders. Ah, the burden, and the slippery pavement, and the constant strain; and yet more sad were the idle groups that looked wistfully at the happy burdened ones.

With a sigh I turned once more homeward, past the monument of the great

London fire, on westward until I reached the Embankment, with its calm and beauty, such a happy contrast to the toilers of London Bridge and its environs, and to the glitter and bustle of the Strand. It was dark once more, the lights gleamed out in their curving lines by the river. Under the arches of Waterloo Bridge, one could get a glimpse, in dim perspective, of the Palace of Westminster and the Abbey. It was all undefined and grand, like some stately music of Beethoven. A livelier measure would typify the Strand, while the titanic sound of storm, or the crashing of the waves upon the shore, might give figure of the toil and labor at London Bridge. Thus my day had contrasts enough, in its almost haphazard flow.

London, January 28, 1872.

XI.

MY second Sunday in London was a busy day. It began with a Celebration at the Abbey at eight o'clock. The morning was wet and gloomy, and, for London the streets almost deserted. It is not far to walk from Northumberland Avenue to Westminster, and wet as the morning was, he would be rather dull who could notice it during such a walk, past Whitehall, where the first Charles shed his blood, past the Horse Guards with all they tell of British martial glory, past Downing Street and all that it hints of political life, and on to the great Abbey itself, looming up in the mist and smoke. We are at the door and enter what seems the empty building. There are perhaps twenty people present, almost unseen in the darkness. At each side of the altar are two standard candles alight, but the lights proper on the altar itself are not lit. Presently, preceded by a verger, there enters a priest who wins my heart at once by his reverent demeanor. Sweetly he utters every word, his soft, clear voice without effort fills the space of the choir. It is a treat to look at him and hear the purity of his English tongue. The great roof above is only dimly visible in the darkness, and down from its unseen depths floats at intervals the cooing of a dove. It comes so weirdly and mystically, like a voice of love from some buried past. Again and again it floats out, possibly not one there noticed it but myself, but I could not help fancying all sorts of things about it. It was my distraction in the service. I thought how fearful it must sound in the empty dark church, and then my longing thoughts went out to the delightful horror of being in the Abbey all alone, and in the dark, and listening to it.

As the service went on I conquered this distraction and when it came time to kneel in that sacred place, I could not keep back the tears. As I turned from the altar with downcast eyes and looked at the rugged pavement, worn by time and many a footstep, I thought of the myriads through all those years, comforted and refreshed there by the Body and Blood of Christ.

At ten o'clock in the morning I was due at St. Mary's Hospital, Paddington, where I assisted the chaplain and made a short address. The hospital is one of the smaller London institutions, but has an enormous number of beds, and was to my eyes a huge affair. The chapel was well appointed and the service choral.

The chaplain kindly piloted me to the nearest interesting church, and selected that one, as he said, "in which Phillips Brooks used to preach"—Christ Church, Lancaster Gate. I found a grand new church, choral Matins and Litany, plain music and good choir, with an enormous congregation. The whole tone was of that splendid style which puts the handsome forward rather than the dogmatic. The altar was vested, had cross and flowers, but no lights, and the reredos and chancel were resplendent with black marble pillars and much color decoration. The preacher was from India, and in his sermon made some startling statements. I remember in particular two of them:

one, that India, under British rule contained one-fifth of the people in the world, the other was that obscene literature, which would not be suffered in England, has freest distribution in India, and that the British government, when asked to prohibit it, decline to do so, for this reason, that if they condemned the obscenity in such literature, they would be condemning similar obscenity existing in the Hindoo religion. Thus, as they cannot by treaty, interfere with the religion of the Hindoos, even indirectly, they are estopped from any action whatever touching the pernicious literature mentioned.

The service over I walked across Kensington Gardens to the Albert Memorial, and in this, my third or fourth view of it, saw more than ever to admire. It is the apotheosis of wifely devotion. Prince Albert in gilt bronze, sits enthroned under a gorgeous canopy of mosaic work, around him are symbolic figures of the arts and sciences, underneath is a great frieze of life size figures, extending round the four sides of the massive base. In this grand series are all the great lights in architecture, painting, sculpture, music and letters. It would be a liberal education to know the life and works of each man there depicted. Twice I walked around the living yet ever still procession, and yet lingering, turned away. A rare skill has been used in the selection and the sculpture. Yet further down the great sweep of steps, at each outer corner, stand a colossal group, representing Europe, Asia, Africa and America, while opposite the whole structure rises the Albert Hall. Getting on top of a bus I got into the neighborhood of my hotel, near Trafalgar Square, and had a little well-earned rest.

Three o'clock found me at the Abbey once more to hear Farrar preach. The choir and transepts were crowded, many standing through the whole service. The usual entrance was so blocked up, that, availing myself of a knowledge of how the land lay, I went round to Poet's Corner and got a good seat opposite the pulpit, though quite out of sight of the singers. This rather gave piquancy to the effect of the music, which was all that one could wish. The sermon was on the ninth Commandment, and such a sermon! It flowed on like a mighty stream, but yet not deep enough to be without broils and rapids. It was a sharp cut against vituperation, while it was in itself a most splendid specimen of the same. The Wesleys and Oliver Cromwell were held up as persecuted saints among a list of others, grouped with like eclecticism. In mentioning also the sufferings of Maurice and Stanley for the truth, they were spoken of as the victims of the "acrid orthodoxy of religious opinion." One could not help thinking of Neale, Keble, Pusey, Newman, and many others.

After the service at the Abbey, Dr. Bridge played gloriously on the great organ, while the congregation flowed out into the nave, walking about, looking at the monuments, or standing in groups listening to the grand music. That over, soon all dispersed.

But the day was not yet over for me. It was dusk, I did not feel tired, and a leisurely stroll down the Embankment toward St. Paul's, where I intended to be at seven o'clock, seemed just the thing. It was pleasant to watch the children at play—the London children, on the one day they can play in the streets without being in danger of their lives. They used their opportunity well.

At last St. Paul's was reached. How solemn and still it all seemed. The church all dark, the streets silent. It was with difficulty I could find a place open to get some tea, but the Faulkner Inn opened its doors, and in a snug little domestic looking coffee-room I made myself comfortable until St. Paul's bells boomed out for service. Quickly the great space of the cathedral was filled up, there must have been at least five thousand present. The choir was that which is called supplementary, the music used was simple, no anthems, but in their place three good congregational hymns; the congregation too sang them with a will. I noticed that whenever the time was not distinct and good the people failed. The first hymn, " O God of hosts, the mighty Lord," had a complicated feeling about its melody; that hymn was poor. " We love the place, O God," with its straight forward tune, had a good swing, but when

Gilbert's setting to " Pleasant are thy courts above," was given out, then there was as the sound of many waters from the assembled throngs; my heart swelled within me as I listened to it.

At last the sermon time has come, and the Hon. E. Lyttleton, headmaster of Haileybury School, ascends the pulpit. He took for his text Job 1:9, " Doth Job serve God for naught?" It was a masterly outline of the Book of Job, and a setting forth of the theme thereof as the inspired answer to modern pessimism. There was grand reserve in the manner of the preacher, a clear far-reaching voice, an intense earnestness, always chastened by severe taste, and a sparing but graceful use of gesture; throughout the length of the masterly discourse, and it was long, the attention of the people seemed unflagging.

I must add that Dean Gregory read the Lessons with a sonorous and sympathetic voice; his heart seemed to go out, in all its genial greatness, with every word, as he gave the Benediction from the altar over that vast congregation at the close.   Slowly they dispersed, and thronged the streets on all sides.   A bus up the Strand brought me comfortably on my way to rest and sleep.

London, January 31, 1892.

XII.

MONDAY morning found us on our way to St. Mary Magdalene's, Munster Square, to attend the funeral of Mr. G. J. Palmer. We felt as undeputed representatives of his many friends in America, who have learned much from the fearless columns of *The Church Times*. We entered after the service had begun, and the tones of the Psalm ringing out well accorded with the draped altar and reredos. All was solemn, sombre and sorrowful. St. Mary Magdalene's is a severe, handsome church, archaic in its form, and especially in its stained glass. How far it is wise, except as a matter of sentimental taste, to revive such severe outlines is a question; such was a flitting thought which impressed itself upon me. At the close of the lesson a hymn was sung and then the solemn Eucharist followed, the music used was the Gregorian Requiem, and lent itself with touching pathos to the occasion. The sequence was the *Dies Iræ*, sung in alternate strains by men and boys. In the latter part of the immortal hymn, the slowness and softness of utterance gave special force and was an illustration of the great effect of such simple music under devout and sympathetic treatment. In the *Agnus Dei* the extremely simple arrangement as found in the requiem music of the Guild of All Souls' was made thrilling by the careful declamation of the boy choristers.

The family of the deceased and immediate relatives alone received. It seemed such a loving, comforting thing to see them approach the altar and also to be especially appropriate that all others who were present should assist them in their loving devotions, and stand aloof in sympathy, not venturing nearer when such sacred grief and blessed personal comfort were upon them.

At the close of the service the choir and officiating clergy grouped themselves around the bier, which was flanked at each side by three tall tapers, the *Nunc Dimittis* was then sung and the coffin censed.

The remaining part of the service was said at the grave in Highgate Cemetery. Thither I went, raining as it was, and in due time reached that city of the dead lifted up above the great city of the living. Had the day been clear the outlook would have been tremendous, but even as it was, one felt the great elevation of the place. The coffin was met at the cemetery gates by choir and clergy, and with solemn song the grave was reached. There amidst a dense down-pour of rain and roaring wind, the last words were said, and George Josiah Palmer was laid to sleep with his kindred. From many hearts went up the prayer that he might rest in peace and that light perpetual might shine upon him. On my way down the steep road which leads to the railway station, I joined myself to a pleasant-looking old gentleman whom I had observed deeply moved at the grave. "Ah," said he, "we were young men together; I remember but as yesterday, when a lot of us, young fellows, took twelve copies of the *Church Times* apiece, just to start it."

I must mention also that just as I was

leaving St. Mary Magdalene's a clergyman addressed me with the question
whether I was not an American and my
name Cooke. Ah, like a flash I could
see it all. He had known my dear friend,
William H. Cooke, dead and gone, once
in Trinity Parish, the genial soul, the
lovely singer, the simple, earnest nature.
Some one had told me once that there
was a touch of resemblance in our faces,
and here this stranger in London stopped
me with the question. We had, you may
be sure, a hearty word of sympathy and
then a loving adieu. Before we parted,
however, he asked once again: "Do you
know Post?" "Yes," said I, "good soul,
he was one of my best friends in the seminary in New York."

From Highgate I made direct by rail
to Moorgate Street station and to my
bankers for letters. Letters from home,
how good they are, and what a delicious
thing to tear them open, devour the con-
tents and then slowly read them all over
again.

My energies being yet good for some
hours' work, I went off into the Whitechapel district, and my luck brought me,

without a thought, to Toynbee Hall and St. Jude's, Whitechapel. As I entered the court of Toynbee Hall, I met the Rev. Mr. Boyle, one of the curates of St Jude's, and in the most courteous way he handed me over to Mr. Aves. Under his direction I had a brief glimpse of this Oxford settlement in East London, and its attempt to plant " sweetness and light " among its grimy denizens. It was not the hour when persons of that class could avail themselves of its benefits. I could see enough, however, from the syllabus of lectures and classes, to learn that a great work was being done, done in a certain way, it is true, but yet done. It was my privilege to see the library with its choice books, to walk through the corridors decorated with engravings and photographs, and to stand in the cheerful dining-room of the resident gentlemen who try to make an evangel of their lives in this crowded part of London. It was a noble room, graced by good pictures, a grand piano, and a full size plaster reproduction of the splendid archer, I think by Thorneycroft. There is nothing harsh or distinctively ascetic, or, indeed, it may

be said, definitely dogmatic about Toynbee Hall, but surely it must do a splendid
work. St. Jude's is close by. It is an
old classical church and every effort has
been made to brighten it up in the esthetic
sense. Engravings and photographs hung
on the pillars, some pictures that looked
like Watts, hung on the wall. One especially impressed me: Love in vain trying
to keep Death, a veiled figure, from en-
tering the portal. There was also a
striking plaster group, life size, of Esau
pleading with Isaac for a blessing. There
was hope in Isaac's face even for
Esau, and so that figure may give
hope to many a modern Esau, who,
too, has sold his birthright for "the
mess of pottage." Slowly I walked
around the church. The old lady care-
taker was putting away all the Bibles and
Prayer Books, for, I think that evening
the Oratorio of the Messiah was to be
sung by a local musical society. I noticed
that the old lady had a nice little gas stove
near her official chair, all aglow. The
font, too, had a cluster of bright red flowers at its foot, and the seats for the choristers in the choir were painted a brilliant

red. What a contrast it all was to St. Mary Magdalene's! It may be that this cheeriness is just what is needed by the poor. Add to it the knowledge of the Faith, and Catholic practice, and you have all wants met.

This constant tendency to cater to the love of pleasure in church matters, leads, one does not know whither; where is it to stop? On coming out a great sign caught my eye on a Baptist church directly opposite: " Commercial Road Baptist church, Free Concerts every Saturday evening, at 8:15." It seems like turning the ways of Zion into a kind of Vanity Fair. Let us hope better results.

I walked on westward by the St. Catherine's Docks and the Tower of London. There was no time to go in. I had seen it all once before, so I contented myself with the grand outside view, over which a great rift in the clouds was shedding a flood of yellowish light. The whole scene looked like an enormous etching by Haden, with its deep browns and flashing lights and intense action. I looked once more at the great White Tower, and the

Traitor's Gate, and then, walking over Tower Hill, turned to the Mark Lane station of the Underground, and was soon thereafter at Charing Cross.

London, February 1, 1892.

XIII.

ON the Feast of the Purification, I made my way to St. Alban's, Holborn, taking my journey from the Strand, through Lincoln's Inn Fields. How little one would expect such expanse, and such quiet nooks, such secluded places, near the clatter and traffic close at hand on the always busy Strand.

One would fain examine those curious places, wander through the magnificent Law Courts, and, if possible, investigate the many Inns of the lawyers, but in the presence of such evident quiet, matter-of-fact company, one dare not intrude, and must be content with looks only, looks which recall all one has read of lawyers and their ways, in Dickens or Thackeray. A little commission I had for a friend, to get him an engraved coat of arms in correct fashion, took me into this neighborhood, where, at the Great Turnstile, I got what was wanted. I had a pleasant chat with the gentleman in charge, who showed me a most interesting collection of heraldic emblazonments in all their fascinating variety. Incidentally I learned that he was on Sundays an organist and choirmaster at a church in Barking, so we had something in common beside the " pomp of heraldry."

It was but a step or so to Brooke Street, Holborn. The Celebration had just begun as I entered St. Alban's. For a week day, there was a good congregation, and the service was all one could desire. The music was rendered by a choir of five men, and some ladies with excellent voices, who were not visible from the congregation. There was a tone of certainty and finish to it, quite refreshing. It was all most elaborate, all except the Introit and Sequence, which were Gregorian.

The ritual at St. Alban's is a matter of careful thought, and the result is shown in a most reverent service. Here, as in other churches I have been in, the men sit on the Epistle side, and the women on the north, or Gospel, side. Here, as in in other particulars, I found perplexing

and needless variations. When at St.
Andrew's, Wells Street, I sat, as I did
elsewhere, on the Epistle side, but in a
short time I was shown the error of my
way by the verger, who ordered me
across the aisle. As one goes about, one
longs for that definite uniformity in ritual
usage which is such a powerful witness
for obedience to authority. In due time
doubtless it will come.

On my way out from St. Alban's, I
visited the Mackonochie Memorial Chapel.
It seemed to me perfect. It is but a small
place, twenty-seven feet eight inches by
sixteen feet four inches, but it has a dignity and a beauty unsurpassed. The exquisite grace and finish of every part take
away the sense of smallness, while the
fullness of detail, the richness of symbolic
allusion in every line, and the graceful
delicacy of the sculptured figures and
varied carvings, convey a sense of at least
spiritual spaciousness, for when there, you
are in the presence of great ideas. A
recumbent white marble figure of Father
Mackonochie is in the sculptor's hands,
as also a beautiful group for the front of
the altar. It is a fitting, and in every

way worthy, memorial of a faithful
priest.

In the afternoon we made a call at
the historic rooms of the Society for the
Propagation of the Gospel, where the
genial secretary, Rev. Mr. Tucker, made
us much at home. I am sure all American clergy visiting London, would find it
pleasant to look in at the central point
of that great force which goes out over
the whole earth, and which in the past
has left its mark upon the Church in
America. I noticed as I passed through
the office, large packing cases with their
tropical-looking tin linings, all marked for
Natal. Delahay Street, where the office
is, is near the Downing Street government mansions. As I left the door, the
rain descended in torrents, and with some
very fine-looking people I took shelter
under one of the great porches, but
bethinking myself of the Abbey close at
hand, and time for Evensong lacking
only ten minutes, I made a dash for that
haven, and got there in time for a glorious service; a splendid anthem from the
Messiah, consisting of the aria, " The
Lord whom ye seek," and the chorus,

" Behold the Lamb of God." Whether the rain or the holiday was the efficient cause of the large congregation, I know not, but large it was. We had a nice clear sermon, also, of about fifteen minutes, on the festival. Still raining at the close, it was convenient to take a bus to Oxford Street, where, alighting near All Saints', Margaret Street, we paid our usual visit to that lovely church, and heard a plain simple Evensong, full of devotion, and sung all through to Gregorian tones. A walk thence by the glittering shops and through the crowded streets, brought us to our hotel home and earned rest.

London, February 2, 1892.

XIV.

WHILE in London I went to a South-west London church for a visit,— St. Andrew's, Stockwell Green. When one gets over Westminster Bridge and takes a tram car it seems like being at home. The cars are American make, brought over here piece-meal, and put together at this side. My friend, the Rev. Mr Everest, pointed out various celebrated spots as we passed along, among them Newman Hall's great meeting-house, with its grand front and spire.

In reaching Stockwell we got out and examined the church of St. John the Divine, Kennington, a beautiful interior of brick, graceful in proportion, with that air of warmth and color so desirable in modern churches. Arrived at Stockwell Green, we enjoyed the charming hospitality of a brother priest and his devoted wife. There we talked over American Church affairs, the election of Bishops, the government of dioceses, the appointments of clergy, the tenure of cure, and all the points of difference which seem so fair and free to our English cousins. I learned on the other hand something of the English side of this Rochester diocese with its seven hundred clergy, of the parish in which I then was, with its seventeen thousand souls, of the manifold forms of work carried on by the priest and his three assistant clergy, and bands of organized workers, in church, Sunday school, day school, and various temperance, literary, and social organizations. It seemed to me such a grand work. After tea we visited a club room for working men, admirably appointed, and presided over by one of the clergy. Here we had chat after chat with one and another, more especially with one dear good lady, who, charmed by our appreciation of London, asked us if we had seen St. Bartholomew's, Smithfield. Of course we had, years ago, and had admired again and again its antique beauty.

From the club we went to the schools where eight hundred children are daily instructed. Here a musical and dramatic entertainment was in full blast, under the direction of a temperance club, and one of the curates acting as director. The school room was crowded with a delighted auditory. There was a farce, and recitations, and music by a brass band. It was amusing enough, but what amused me most was the extreme difficulty to catch the words, because of the soft intonations and curious elisions of vowels and consonants.

I was perhaps a little hard in steadily refusing to say something, but I was a looker on, and glad to study this little glimpse of work in a crowded district in South-west London.

After leaving London I came directly to Nottingham, not much affected by pleasure travel, but a commercial centre of much importance in manufactories, and interesting to me, from family associations.

Nottingham itself has a few remnants of mediæval times, notably its three great churches of St. Mary, St. Peter, and St. Nicholas, the former, a grand cathedral-like building in the perpendicular style of architecture. The castle, too, on its great crag, reminding one of Edinburgh, accents the whole place with a historic tone. The sinuous streets with here and there old English fronts outside, and panelled oak within, attract attention. The place is noted for its great central market place, where, especially on Saturdays, one may find a busy scene indeed, everything possible on sale—fish, flesh and fowl, with all sorts of commodities you can imagine. The part of the market given up to flowers was particularly attractive. I was much pleased with the tasteful arrangement of the stalls, and the appreciative selection of ivy, laurel, and other shrubs, as well as harmonious groups of choicer plants.

In my wandering about among the booths and in the streets, I came on an old darkey selling papers. Having bought one I got into conversation with him, and soon learned from him in the soft full voice of the genuine darkey, that he had shipped from New Haven fifteen years before, and that he had been in Nottingham ever since. When I asked him if he ever wanted to go back to America, " No, sah," said he, " I can lay my bones

heah, as well as theah, I am as neah to
Him." There was a touching trust in
his poor old face, and a humble content
worth imitating.

Lenton, Nottingham, February 5, 1892.

XV.

I HAVE come from a most interesting experience here in Nottingham. It was in an immense warehouse where lace curtains are finished and put upon the market in all parts of the world; where the finer sorts of laces are produced in splendid imitation of old point, in all its historical varieties, which I am not learned enough to name; where all manner of dainty nicknacks in trimmings are turned out by machinery which almost seems to think; to this immense establishment I was driven for the opening of the day at 8:30 A. M., and what do you suppose was this beginning? It was the united prayers and praises of employers and employed, all together, some five hundred of them, in a well-appointed chapel, with good organ, choir, and choral service. It was a most delightful thing to hear that multitude sing with lusty voices, "The

King of Love, my Shepherd is. His goodness faileth never."

From the platform I watched them all as they came in, quietly, briskly, orderly, and then there was in so many instances, the reverent bowing down for silent prayer. Men, women, and girls, altogether in that great chapel in the basement of the huge warehouse. It was a lovely sight. The service book is a compilation from the Book of Common Prayer, a varying portion being taken for each day; addresses are added on Tuesdays and Thursdays, but the whole service is kept within half an hour. The service this morning consisted of a hymn, a few collects, the decalogue with responses, and the prayer for Christ's Church Militant, the address, and benediction.

It was my privilege to give the address, and few occasions ever gave me such pleasure. I had heard the service in St. George's, Windsor; in St. Paul's, and the Abbey, but nowhere did it seem so thrilling as uttered by those work people before their daily toil.

It certainly is a happy idea to assem-

ble all as a great family before the duty
of the day begins. The working people
take a deep interest in the services; they
have themselves paid for the organ, and
look upon employment in this warehouse
as a distinct advantage. I have been told
that a well-defined, refining influence, is
marked in all employed there; and certainly it seemed so, as one saw the intelligent, refined and cultivated faces among
them.

One of the proprietors with a just
pride told me that I would be astonished
to find the advancement, intelligence, and
varied information which existed among
them. I need hardly say that it would
not have surprised me in the least, for I
have found full many a beautiful blossom
in humble, lowly places, and much innate
refinement under most unfavorable circumstances. Said my friend: I had a
lady visitor from London, and a Board
meeting kept me so busy that I could not
just at the moment give the interview
required. In my predicament I bethought
me of one of the girls in the packing
room to amuse my grand visitor from
the metropolis. "Get a cab," said I to

the girl, " and take this lady to the Castle Museum or anywhere you like, and entertain her until I have leisure. So," said he, " I left the two together, the lady in sealskin, and the factory girl in her own simple garb. When I returned, I found them hob-nobbing together in splendid style, the lady having accepted an invitation to share the factory girl's tea in the refreshment hour. Afterwards I had a note from the lady's husband thanking me for the splendid time his wife had on her visit. It was none of my doing, it was the intelligent and genial companionship of the factory girl." I felt myself that this bright spirit extended on all hands, as I went with my friend from floor to floor, being shown by the employees in the various departments, the specialties over which they each had control.

I must add that two chaplains and an organist are engaged for the daily services, and duly paid by the company. Surely it is a good investment and one that might well be copied in our many mammoth enterprises of Chicago.

Lenton, Nottingham, February 9, 1892.

XVI.

WHAT can exceed the unaffected hospitality of an English home? There is a delicious quiet about it, a matter-of-fact gentle assumption that you are completely at home, and that you are thus also completely at ease. You come and go at your own will, under the sole obligation to be present at the culmination of the day, the seven o'clock dinner. You are free for all else. Your own room, with easy chair and well-supplied writing table, may be your retreat, or you can enjoy library or drawing-room, or the pleasures of the park or garden. A gentle, unvarying attention is paid by the silent and noiseless servants. Your every want is quietly anticipated. You may return after a drive in the chilly air — a bright coal fire in your room will greet you there, while your slippers, laid where you can easily get them, also give welcome. The house

is all happily-innocent of water pipes or
stationary wash-basins, but hot water will
be sure to be on hand for your dinner
toilet, and ere you are up in the morning
a great brass pitcher of the same cheering temperature will be brought to your
door, with which, and a sitting bath tub
in your room, you can make a most comfortable beginning to your day. If you
get to the breakfast room before nine,
doubtless you will be first there yourself,
but soon the head of the house and others
arrive, the servants come in for family
prayers, I have seen six of them, Bible in
hand, comely women and maids, a goodly
sight, fair, well dressed and neatly capped.

That family worship, morning and
night, that daily round of Scripture reading, that constant recurrence of portions
of the Book of Common Prayer, how
"good and how pleasant" it is all!

What a lovely, straggling meal breakfast is! Your letters are by your plate;
after grace is said everybody reads and
eats as he chooses. "What will you
have? Help yourself; there are chops,
sardines on toast, and cold venison." So
you go to the side-board and have a slice

of what you want. Then plans are made for the day. "A carriage will be at the door for Bisley at half after eleven," or "We go calling in the afternoon," or "There is a walking party out to some historic site or another later on."

You must be dull, indeed, if, when, dressed for dinner, you take your place in the drawing room, you have not had a happy day, and have also a keen, good appetite for the good things which await you, and the lovely hours which follow thereafter until prayers and bedtime. At last the candles are brought, and once more alone before a cheerful fire in your spacious, simply-furnished, but most comfortable room, you prepare yourself for sweet sleep and pleasant dreams.

One day recently I made a special pilgrimage to Clumber, the seat of his Grace, the Duke of Newcastle, to see the beautiful church which he has recently erected for the use of his household, close to his castle gates.

The way led me for eighteen miles across country, through village after village, each with its venerable church and clustering cottages of red tiled roofs.

Pleasant it was to dash along the well-kept roads, by farm house and ploughed field, over hill and dale, and at last enter the beautiful parks which lead on to Clumber. The first of these was Rufford, glorious with Scotch firs, old beeches, and lustrous evergreens. After-ward came Thoresby, the seat of Lord Manvers, a noble expanse of forest and rich woodland, part of Sherwood Forest; great troops of deer were on every side, while pheasants and other game con-stantly broke covert. At last Clumber was reached, a great pile of buildings without special architectural attraction, but filled, we were told, with objects of art. Somehow I never care for a hurried look at such matters. It is a most tiring operation, and an outrage on one's artistic conscience. My coachman rather startled me by asking if I wished to drive up to the front door. "No," said I. "I am sure the Duke would be glad to see me, but really I have not the honor of his acquaintance." At this juncture a passing retainer, evidently ready to be inter-viewed, informed us that if we wished to see the church we should drive up to it, and ask for the verger, Mr. Harvey. This we did, but every door was locked. The external beauty made one long all the more for that which was within. In this fix we bethought us of the chaplain, and went to his residence. The kindly spoken servants told us with regret that he was away and would not be home until night, suggesting to us that we should see the Duke's housekeeper who could possibly open the church for us. We soon saw this good lady; cheery and bright she was, in her great apartment which was covered with family pictures and filled at one side with an immense cabinet crowded with rare old china. Back we went with her to the parson's house where after a little search she found his keys, and opened for us the church doors.

It is, without exception, the most stately and harmonious small church I have ever seen. I could only take a regretfully rapid glance over the whole place, and take in the general effect, for I had yet to drive back eighteen miles to reach home.

I entered at the side door, a little, narrow affair, but at once went down the nave to the western entrance to get the impression, first, of the whole building. The church is cruciform, a nave with choir, and transepts, and choir aisles. The south choir aisle contains the Lady chapel; the north choir aisle, the organ chamber, and vestry rooms. The interior and exterior are done in warm-tinted stone, like our Lake Superior sandstone; the windows are placed high, and the open roof, exquisite in proportion. The whole place has such a satisfying, harmonious effect —glass, woodwork, carved stone, ornaments, everything — that the eye is diverted from detail. One gets an impression of a small interior, magnificent in itself, commanding reverent admiration as a whole. You look through the open door of the choir screen and see the altar, glorious in itself and white with its six lights and other groups of tapers! It is splendidly vested, and rich in every ornament, the cross, the tabernacle, the candlesticks, faultless in taste and workmanship. Back again the eye is drawn to the screen. I only have an impression of rich wood carving, with saints, and angels, and sacred symbols over all. What attracted me most was a unique looking rood, with the Blessed Virgin and St. John, an elaborate piece of carving, hanging suspended over the screen itself, while on the screen stood six immense candlesticks holding tall wax tapers.

The nave and side chapel were seated with plain chairs; all were alike, the Duke and his family having no other distinction than that of being in the front row.

The north transept was occupied by a beautifully carved confessional, and the south transept by the font.

After this hurried glance at the whole building from the nave, I entered the Lady chapel. The red light told me the sacrament was reserved upon the altar.

From thence I went to the high altar in the choir. Here the housekeeper removed the antependium and disclosed the sculptures in the altar front, done in purest white marble.

The choir stalls are cedar and, I think, mahogany. Every bench-end, every panel, is a study and a lesson, Saints, and prophets, and martyrs, angels and arch-angels, all are there in loveliest form; hangings of choicest velvet, lovely tints of blue and green, with subdued ornaments of flower and fruit, all are combined in the daintiest and most perfect fashion for this church of St. Mary the Virgin at Clumber. From it, with all its beauty, my mind turned to St. Mary's, Burlington, New Jersey, the creation of Bishop Doane. The same cruciform shape, the same rich tint of stone, the same great central spire, and if not the same in beauty, at least under the same invocation to St. Mary, and witness to the same love.

The drive home was even more pleasant than our coming, for the keen north-easter was to our backs, and beauties of wood and field not seen before made themselves evident. Both journeys were brightened by the sweet hospitalities of a charming home, where we tarried for luncheon and for tea. That was a happy hour we had turning over the leaves of an illustrated book on horses and dogs with an enthusiastic young sportsman not

yet out of petticoats.   Happy home,
happy children, splendid drive, and glorious church at Clumber, the point of our
pilgrimage.

Southwell, Nottingham, February 13, 1892.

XVII.

ONE of my Sundays at Nottingham
gave me the opportunity to attend
at St. Mary's, the great church of the
town.   It was a little late when I entered, and as I was ushered up to a good
seat by the verger, I could hear the great
booming, earnest, though indistinct tones
of the people joining in the *Te Deum*.
They looked happy, pleased, and devotional.

St. Mary's is a great cruciform structure, largely in the perpendicular Gothic,
which gives such an air of light, and
almost fantastic display of windows. The
whole of the transepts seem to be glass,
divided by a trellis work of latticed stone.
Such work impresses me as the product
of a rich imagination held in check by
rule.   It will display its vigor and richness but in an exquisite order and propriety.   We have not, that I know of, in
America a good specimen of this style.

Would that we had! It seems to make the very stones breathe the life of exuberant, joyous faith, and the walls to let in the lustre of the spiritual world.

Canon Richardson was the preacher, a man gifted with precise, incisive speech, and that chastened manner indicative of reserve power.

The service consisted of choral Matins, simply chanted, an anthem, the sermon, and offertory verse; all was over in an hour and a quarter. This is paving the way for better things, and the service of services — a full choral Eucharist for worship—Communions having been made beforehand, at the Celebration which each priest ought to say at least every Sunday. Three priests are the usual staff in these churches; this would give two early Celebrations, and a High Celebration, with priest, deacon, and sub-deacon at the usual hour of a quarter to eleven in the morning.

One must respect "the patience of the saints" which one meets with in England and elsewhere. You will find thorough knowledge, noble courage, earnest desire for full Catholic truth and practice, and

with it all, this saintly patience with
utter opposites, this gentle submission to
apparently inevitable circumstances, this
prayerful hopefulness that in God's good
time all will be well, this humble witness
where God has placed them in His good
providence.

I never tire of those vast English congregations, and their ecclesiastically speak-
ing, heterogeneous flood. In they stream
to the church, some heedless, though
quiet and reserved; others devout and
exact, as others are apparently careless.
All are in the church — and side by side
— and worshipping. And then, after
service, the flood rolls out in like manner; "all sorts and conditions of men,"
almost in every sense of the word.

In the afternoon of this day, it was
my pleasant duty to go out to a village
church in Derbyshire, and preach there
at the evening service, making an appeal
for the restoration fund of the building.
It was in the little village of Sawley, a
quiet little place without mills or machinery, or any modern innovation that I
could descry.

The rambling street was a picture,

each house with an expression of its own, like a row of rustic heads, no two alike, but all quaint, irregular, and interesting. Red roofs, straw roofs, queer chimneys, oddly placed windows, crumbling stone and brick, all covered with glints and tints of moss and stain of time.

The church turned out to be a lovely old building, consisting of a good nave with pillared aisles, a long drawn choir, separated by an ancient wooden screen. The stalls and it were of oak, black with age and use. There were some curious recumbent figures, and many tombs pathetic in their mutilation.

The whole place was to me a text on which to string memories of the Church, from its first foundation on that spot more than one thousand years ago, and of hopes for the future, as one looked at the splendid restoration already accomplished there, and elsewhere, and of the grand outlook for the whole Church in the English-speaking empire and the vast continent of the United States. Was it too much to dream that in some future congress of the English race, from all parts of the earth, America and the English

Empire would be one in confederation, and England be a Holy Land, a place of shrines to which all English hearts would turn " from the rising of the sun even unto the going down thereof ? "

The drive out from Nottingham to Sawley was through village after village, each with its well-appointed church and comely churchyard. My heart ached as I thought of the vast stretches of our own land, sadly lacking in such splendid equipment for teaching to all men the knowledge of salvation. Few and far between are our country churches, so that with us it may be that pagan will have again its double meaning. But God forbid! The drive home was in the quiet of the night, with the stars looking down exactly as they beamed upon me in Chicago, so minute is the little arc of separation here below, compared with the vast sweep of the stars above.

I may mention that the offertory was about fifty dollars, and the wholesome-faced rustic wardens asked me to come again.

I must also add that the choir was quite creditable, a great contrast musically, it is true, to others I had heard; but what was lacking in art was evidently made up for in heart, for men and boys alike seemed fully impressed with the importance of their work.

Lenton, Nottingham, February 28, 1892.

XVIII.

ASH Wednesday has come and gone. It found me in Oxford, and left me after a day of blessed quiet and profit. The silence and seclusion of a religious house came with special sweetness at such a time. The awaking at an early hour, the united prayers, the solemn Eucharist, so reverential and so simple, in that upper room, duly prepared, the retreat of one's own cell, the various calls to prayer, the awful earnestness of the Litany and Commination service in the parish church, the august simplicity and splendid power of the sermon, not one word for effect, but every syllable for truth and practice, all make up an ideal time of refreshing.

I had never heard the Commination Service before. The Preface sounds out with an old-time air thus: "Brethren, in the Primitive Church there was a godly discipline, that, at the beginning of Lent, such persons as stood convicted of

notorious sin were put to open penance,
and punished in this world, that their souls
may be saved in the day of the Lord;
and that others, admonished by their ex-
ample, might be the more afraid to
offend." It is a heart-searching service,
and as read and sung by the aged priest,
had in it a grand ring of authority and
power. The *Miserere* is sung at its close
alternately by priest and people. The
voice of the officiant unaccompanied by
the organ, quavered off in its imperfect
but most earnest manner, undisturbed by
the mechanical accuracy of organ pipes;
it was most touching, the full voices of
choir, people, and organ, making the
response. Here, I may say, that the
Church rule which prescribes that the
organ should not accompany the priest's
voice in collects, prefaces, and versicles,
seems founded upon common sense. If
the voice is old and cracked, but venerable, and beloved, and, above all other
relations, necessary, as the voice of the
officiant, then an impertinent organ part,
with its own most positive imperfections,
only increases the difficulty, marring the
solemnity, and not mending the music. I

might also add that there are powers of fine gradation in the well-trained expressive voice, which are unattainable by organ pipes.

In the evening at eight, Knox-Little preached at St. Barnabas', the first of a course of conferences on Social Questions of the day. The great church was packed with people — it will hold fifteen hundred — on one side a solid body of men, undergraduates the most of them, and undergraduate Oxford represents the hope and flower of English life. I sat away back, near the door; one's heart thrilled to look out over such a congregation, and to note the earnestness, devotion, spirit, and manliness· of such a crowd. On the other side were women, many of them, too, engaged in literary pursuits, and all deeply interested in the great cause of religion, which in Oxford finds at once its greatest conflicts, greatest victories, and greatest opportunities.

St. Barnabas', Oxford, has been my ideal of a town church, one that might have been, and in God's good time may yet be, in Chicago. It was built by Mr. Coombe, University printer, long since gone to his reward. The structure is what one might call inexpensive, for though cheap, there is nothing cheap-looking about it. It is a Basilica, a plain parallelogram, a great pillared oblong space, with side aisles, and an apse at the east end in which stands the high altar under a grand canopy. In front of the altar, extending out into the nave, stands the choir, raised, and enclosed by open screen work. The structure is of concrete, trimmed with brick, plain and severe in form, but made elegant by correct lines, well chosen ornament, and tasteful color and gilding. A fine campanile stands at the south-east corner, affording in its lower story adequate vestry and choir rooms; above, a place for the organ and a full chime of tubular bells.

The effect of a highly gilded altar, the covering baldachino, the choir enclosed and elevated, as seen through the vista of a pillared nave, is exceedingly rich and magnificent. In the apse roof above the altar is a colossal figure of our Lord in glory seated, in the Byzantine style. In front of the apse, are the symbols of the four Evangelists, two at each side. The

distant altar, the many lights, the choir in
its place, and the vast kneeling throng of
men and women, made a scene long to be
remembered.

It was lovely to hear the grand volume of sound, as the hymn, " Weary of
earth and laden with my sin," rolled out
from all those hearts; a friend with me
was singing bass; I said: " Sing the air;
all are singing it," which at once he did.
It seemed impertinent to take another
part than the very soul itself, the distinctive melody. In such congregational singing there was a certain assertion, and at
the same time a certain vagueness which
belongs to real art, there was a positive
form, but with it a blending of outline
which eluded the ear, as the same quali-
ties in a picture give pleasure to the eye.

Of Knox-Little's preaching what can I
say! Years have passed since I last heard
him. A certain tender interest attaches
to the moment when such a man appears
before you once again. Was he changed?
Will he preach as well? I hope he is as
powerful as ever. These are the thoughts
which leap through the mind as he
ascends the pulpit, as he kneels for

prayer, as he stands before you. Yes, there he was, the same slight figure, but a little increased in bulk; the same black hair, but tonsured by the advancing years; the same earnest face; but above all the same grand sympathetic voice. Powerfully it rang out as the text was uttered: "Blow the trumpet in Zion, sanctify a fast, call a solemn assembly." For an hour he held us in his hands. He showed us glimpses of the great questions of the day, of the duty and responsibility of the Church regarding them, and of our personal share in the whole matter. A thrilled hush was over that congregation as the speaker came to the close of his impassioned peroration. I can remember none of it, but the effect of the whole is with me, capped and climaxed with the utterance of the last word in ecstatic tones, the Name of names, "Jesus."

There was no concluding hymn or blessing from the altar; the preacher himself, after a moment's pause, gave the benediction from the pulpit, and all was over. I rather liked this way. Here and there were kneeling figures, moved by the impassioned words, while the vast throng moved out with the impression of the sermon fresh and undisturbed in their hearts.

It was a grand ending of my Ash Wednesday.

Oxford, March 2, 1892.

XIX.

I ATTENDED, by invitation, a meeting of the Church Congregational Music Association, held at the Church House, in Dean's Yard, Westminster, one day last week. Church House, as yet, is the fine old mansion now occupying the site hereafter to be covered by a more ecclesiastical pile. When the whole west end of Dean's Yard is duly filled with the projected magnificent building, it will be a worthy addition to that classic locality. How quaint and black and dingy Dean's Yard appears. You look across at the unpretending front, and see where the Dean of royal Westminster lives, and you rather rejoice that Archdeacon Farrar has a handsome Gothic bay window to look out of, and let in all that can be got of light, out of the grey London air.

I was welcomed by the genial secretary, Mr. Griffiths, who remarked that though I had furtherest to come — from

Chicago — I was *first* there. We soon had our meeting in full blast, presided over by Bishop Mitchinson, who remembered me, after the lapse of, perhaps, twenty years, since I visited him in Canterbury. The report read gave an encouraging outlook for this young society. The Bishop made an admirable address on the great need of reform in our Church music, and several took part most interestingly, in the discussion.

There are several difficulties in the way of Church congregational music, much as it is to be desired. The first and chiefest is, that to take part in Matins or Evensong, one must be able to turn the book readily, that is, find the places, and then there must be the power to read fluently and well, otherwise it will not be possible to take part even in the Psalter, when read, and much less when sung. An unvarying set of Sunday Psalms thoroughly well known, like the *Venite* or Canticles, might be learned, but the recurring Psalms for the day present difficulties to the ordinary worshipper. The speed, too, of the chanting, with intricate harmonies and melodies, all are hindrances. I have never yet heard a clear, good congregational rendering of a chant; the nearest approach to it is the occasional singing of our own traditional *Gloria in Excelsis* as rendered by large bodies of voices in our conventions. This is slow, well known, and of simple harmonic construction, and limited range. I have recently looked over a book of new tunes here, and not five in the volume were capable of congregational rendering. They were one succession of suspended harmonies, stimulating to a jaded professional ear, but confusing utterly to the simple layman in the divine art. It was an absolute relief to play over such a tune as St. Ann's, and feel the solid swing of its clear melody and straightforward harmony. People can sing such tunes taken with lots of good, loud organ, a grave, steady well-marked time, and no fancy expression.

People speak of the grand effect of the German chorale. It is got in this very way. The organist pulls out all his stops, the tune is familiar, the time slow, and the people sing in unison. Here is perhaps the real *crux*. English people, and

Americans also, love to sing in harmonies. Let them do so, I say, but let the
harmonies be as simple as possible, and
always related to the diatonic scale. I
was in St. Mary's, Nottingham, last Sunday evening — a noble church, and grand
congregation. Only in one chant was the
effect full, for the people tried to sing, and
that was a simple chant to *Nunc Dimittis*,
by Blow, in E minor. That chant was
joined in all over the church, while the
others, intricate and involved, were merely
muttered by the people. So in the hymns,
"Jesus, lover of my soul" was taken too
fast, and the last hymn, to a simple,
though sentimental tune, was joined in
heartily. The Communion service properly and simply set, forms the best basis
for congregational singing, because the
principal parts never vary, that is, the
Kyrie, Credo, Sanctus, etc., and *Gloria
in Excelsis*. The responses, likewise, are
always the same.

In all Church services the choir, as
such, is a necessary adjunct, even if the
choir be represented by one acolyte.
Hence, a really perfect service ought to
have priest, choir, and people, in active

co-operation. I believe something like the following plan would improve our services in a congregational aspect:

Let the opening part of Matins or Evensong be taken on a low note, and in unison, responses and all, to end of *Venite*. Let the Psalms be chanted, not choirwise, but by a single voice in the odd verses, answered by the full choir in the even verses. Let the congregation follow as they can, the full body of sound answering the single voice will give courage for their effort; but let all join in the recurring *Gloria Patri*, the organist making due pause for this united outburst of praise. I heard this effect produced at the Festival Service in St. Paul's when the full orchestra joined in with the choir, at the end of each recurring Psalm. On that occasion the Psalms were sung by the Cathedral Choir alone; other choirs present, with the orchestra, joining only in the *Gloria Patri*. Had the people been instructed to be silent in the Psalter, until each oft-repeated *Gloria Patri*, the effect would have been sublime. This plan recognizes, too, the grace of listening devoutly to Church music; for

I am confident that the silent reading
of the Psalms by the people as they are
sung by the choir, is a most spiritual
exercise and meditation, the recurring
Gloria sung by all, comes then with
heart and soul. The *Te Deum* and Canticles might be sung in like fashion, but
as the *Te Deum* ends with the odd verse,
"O Lord, in Thee, etc.," that verse might
be well repeated by entire congregation
and choir, like the ancient *pneuma*. Four
simple settings of the *Credo*, of which
Merbecke should be one, would give
variety and stability to the Communion
service; *Sanctus* might follow the same
rule, while the *Agnus* and *Benedictus*
might be left generally to the choir.

One must recognize that choirs are a
necessary adjunct of divine service; congregational music must not usurp their
place, while ample opportunity for congregational music must be given by
choirs in stately, well marked, simple
hymns, chants, and responses.

Oxford, March 5, 1892.

XX.

MY first Sunday in Oxford, this visit, gave me such pleasure that I must give in detail its many delights. It opened with an early Celebration at St. Barnabas, where was a goodly number of communicants, and a reverent service. I hoped to have attended the later Celebration at this church, when Fr. Maturin was to be the preacher, but the historic Bampton Lecture at the historic St. Mary's, proved too strong a counter attraction. To St. Mary's then, I went, and was fortunate enough to meet one of the Heads of Houses at the door, who saw that I had an excellent seat, in a priviledged place, near the pulpit.

There are few more interesting sights in Oxford than the delivery of those Bampton Lectures. Each annually recurring course witnesses to the generous spirit of the Rev. John Bampton, canon of Salisbury, who founded them many

years ago. The scene in itself is ever
fresh and attractive. The church of St.
Mary the Virgin, Oxford, is divided by
the organ screen into choir and nave.
The latter is essentially a preaching
place; a great gallery occupies the west
end and north side; here the undergraduates sit, a goodly company — to me, ever
a fair sight, pathetic and inspiring in its
outlook and prospects. Underneath the
galleries, and in every available space,
are seats for whoever can get them, while
the great nave space is set apart for the
college dons of various grades. In the
center of the north side of the nave, facing the south, is a high seat for the vice-
chancellor; and directly opposite is the
historic pulpit, where the best brain of
Oxford has stood up to teach from that
" Word " whose open page is blazoned
on the arms of the university: *Dominus
illuminatio mea.* Silently and quietly,
as English congregations can do so well,
sit that great assembly, awaiting the
formal entrance of the vice-chancellor,
the distinguished Officers of Oxford, the
preacher of the day, and their retinue.
Looking down on the great throng from

the choir screen, are the little choristers whose duty it is to lead the singing. They are to help in the highest function of all, higher than even a Bampton Lecture, which is the praise and glory of God; but their sweet young faces show no consciousness of their mission; haply they know it not, and in this, their innocent ignorance, may they not approach the unimpassioned service of the very angels?

At last the silence and our own brooding thoughts are broken by the rising of all from their seats as the procession enters, heralded by vergers and others.

All are clad in their robes of office, but in grave black. As it is Lent, the gorgeous red gowns are not used, such as once I saw in summer term, when years ago I heard Pusey preach.

The preacher on this occasion is Bishop Barry. He at once enters the pulpit; all kneel for a silent prayer, and stand to sing that hymn which always moves me: " Rock of ages cleft for me." It rolls out grandly, swelled by the vast mass of men's voices. I sing away on the first verse, but as I listen to the second in its great subdued fullness, I cannot restrain my tears. How glorious is congregational melodic singing as sung by men! It is like Wagnerian brasses, doing what nothing else can do. There is no other service but the reading by the preacher of the quaint Bidding Prayer, a lovely relic of the past, ever fresh and fitting for these times. All the petitions for which we are to pray are recounted duly, and then, all kneeling, is said that sum of all prayers, " Our Father."

The line of thought indicated by the preacher was, that as the Law was a schoolmaster to bring us to Christ, so science with its law was a servant to bring us to the knowledge of a living One, the incarnate God.

I sometimes think that this constant battle and apology — well enough in a lecture and in a place like this Oxford — seems sadly out of place in the average pulpit; one does hear too much of it everywhere. The general open teaching of the Church should always be positive dogma and definite detail as to duty. This is the shepherd's work, to provide food and indicate due restraint.

Bishop Barry uttered his lecture in

grand style. There were many noble passages; perhaps if fault there was, it was that all was on one splendid height. It kept me closely interested for its hour, and then the benediction from the pulpit dismissed us all.

From St. Mary's, down the "High," over Magdalen Bridge I went, and on to Cowley Iron church. We entered as Father Hall was concluding his sermon, and found ourselves in time for the latter part of the choral Celebration. There was no pause after Christ's Church Militant prayer here, and a reverent congregation heartily joined through all, to the close. I hope I shall see the new church built at Cowley. The old Iron church has many tender memories, but a proper setting for such services and such preaching is sadly needed. The grand site on Iffley Road stands ready for occupancy, and I am sure that American Churchmen owe many a debt to Father Hall and the Society of St. John the Evangelist, which offerings for the new church here would gracefully acknowledge. Of the dinner succeeding at Cowley, of the sweet free hours in the common room, where Fathers Page, Maturin, and Hall, were present, with many others; of the hours in the chapel, of the pleasant chat resumed again in the library, I can but give a glimpse, and pass on at once to our afternoon walk to Iffley church.

The whole sky was overcast with indigo clouds, giving a tender light upon the brown landscape, just the setting for that gray tower and antique church, dating from King Stephen. The vicar met us within the walls, and pointed out the rich Norman arches, and all the other features of this quaint building. But old as the church was, the hoary life of the great yew tree in the churchyard seemed more awful and venerable. How sweet it was to wander among the graves, pale with snowdrops, and here and there gleaming with the joyous gold of the crocus. Having to be back to Oxford for Evensong at five, we soon turned our steps thitherward. The trees, the cottages, the clouds, the distant tender lines of the landscape, the rosy children by the wayside, the peaceful groups of people out for a walk like ourselves, the quaint, gnarled old couple in the comical

old cart drawn by a most diminutive don-
key, all gave us something to look at,
and laugh at too, perhaps, until we were
once more at Magdalen Bridge, and
turned in at New College, where we
heard Evensong in grandest Anglican
style.

But before doing this we had a lovely
turn or two in the college gardens, to
occupy our time until the chapel was
open; lovely spot, with the old ivy-
covered walls of mediaeval Oxford form-
ing its boundary on one side, and the
great Gothic pile of the college buildings
the other, while in the midst are stately
trees and evergreens, green sward and
flower beds, where fairy primroses are
asleep, waiting for the sunshine to kiss
them into life.

The service was the splendid and
sombre Walmsley in D minor, spoiled for
me because I was under the organ in the
ante-chapel. The anthem was from Mendelssohn, including "If with all your
hearts," and the quartette, "Cast thy
burden upon the Lord," all sung angelic-
ally. The best part of the service was
the hymn, "When I survey the won-

drous cross," sung after Evensong by the choir and all the students. This was followed by the blessing, and this again by Stainer's sevenfold Amen, sung, I do think, even better than at St. Paul's; and so, after that solemn hush which follows such deep emotions, the organ thundered forth, and all the students, clergy, and others, surpliced as they were, crowded out into the ante-chapel, sitting about to listen to the concluding music of the great organ.

A quiet evening, after all this day, was enjoyable. Even Father Hall, preaching in a church near by, could not entice us out from our fireside. Cold as the outer air was, we could not help opening our windows as the night wore on, to let in the clangor of the bells from the tower of St. Giles's near by, which in their many changes from half past eight to after nine o'clock, seemed to bid us a musical good night.

Oxford, March 6, 1892.

XXI.

A DAY in Oxford brings with it many delights. I know not of any place which so satisfies a reflective nature, one that can be touched with the glory of the past, the vigor of the present, and the splendid promise of the future.

We rambled about, my friend and I, and cunningly he would bring me to points of picturesque advantage, where on either hand some graceful piece of architecture would emphasize the vista. One such lovely spot is to stand on the " High," opposite the Schools Building, and see on one hand St. Mary's spire and on the other the lovely tower of Magdalen College, with the graceful sweep of the noblest street in Europe stretching in between.

Another such was to stand outside of Canterbury gate, at the corner of Merton Lane and Oriel Lane, with Merton

Tower on one hand and St. Mary's spire once more on the other.

Again what a charm it was to watch the glimpses of the colleges as seen, now in one grouping, now in another yet more beautiful than before, framed in by the noble trees, or in combination with each other, and more humble, but ever picturesque, structures of Oxford.

We went calling from college to college, in through quadrangle after quadrangle, under time-worn arches, into rooms piled high with books, brooded over by gentle ease and persistent application and steadfast, unselfish work.

Our afternoon's calling done, we passed through Christ Church, and down the meadow walk to the river, where a boat race was to come off at half past four. The day was a trifle chilly, snow flakes were in the air, but that did not deter the thinly-clad and bare-kneed students from their sport. Bright and fresh they looked as they crowded the barges, gay with bunting, and trooped along the banks on either side. The crews dropped down the river in their slender shells to the starting point, and soon the beginning of

the race was announced by the enthusiastic shouts of the impetuous crowd,
cheering the onward speeding crafts.
On the boats came in grand style, while
the excited students on the shore kept
even pace, urging their favorites by
enthusiastic shouts.

The sky was an English winter sky,
but the over-hanging clouds were not
without their beauty. The curving
stream, the dashing boats, the gay colors
flying, the crowd of generous and splendid fellows absorbed in the vigor of the
effort, made a charming picture. When
all was over, the crowd trickled off
through the winding paths and up the
meadow walk, adding continued interest
to ever attractive Oxford.

In the evening, we went to St. Barnabas to hear the first of a series of Lent
lectures by Father Maturin. There was
the same crowd as on Ash Wednesday,
earnest and attentive. The service consisted of a Litany of Repentance, sung
kneeling, a hymn, and the sermon, and
such a sermon! But first, I must tell of
Father Maturin. He looks well and
strong, and it seems to me that his voice

is more rich and full than ever. A hush
fell over that congregation as he gave
out his text in the mellowest of tones,
but thrilling to the very core: "What
I would, that do I not; but what I hate,
that I do."

For nearly an hour he kept us stilled
with beating hearts, as he showed us ourselves in our sinning freedom, and in our
almost despairing remorse at the sins
which we do, but hate; and then with
sympathetic and gentlest words, he
showed us how we may do better,
through love of Him in whose strength
we could battle on and on against our
faults. I never heard a sermon which
more forcibly showed the inside of one's
heart, the struggles and despairs of experience, or which sounded out in such
trumpet-tones the necessity for effort, and
the assurance of victory to all who strive
to follow in love the teachings of the
Master.

One short Collect and the benediction
from the pulpit, pronounced with pathetic
tenderness over that deeply-moved audience, brought all to a close.

What follows is not germane to the

foregoing, but it may as well be said here as elsewhere.

One often finds in England such hazy views about the American Church, and this in most unexpected quarters, that one longs to give to our brethren, juster notions and wider conceptions as to our mission in the United States.

To a true Churchman, no condition of the Church since the time of Constantine presents a more interesting study than our position in America; a Church absolutely free from State control, in the usual sense of that idea, witnessing in the most primitive fashion for the verities of the Faith and the divine constitution of the Church, in the face of the newest development of material progress and assertion. Ours are the problems of the first centuries, to win in later times a new world for Christ.

Surely in this central Oxford there ought to be some witness of that mission of the American Church, some central bureau of information which would be ready and able to disseminate such information, and some opportunity of showing the Church existing as separated from governmental attachment, entirely and absolutely a spiritual creation. Ought there not to be here some representative institution of the American Church, itself witnessing to its character, its mission, its works, and its progress? With these thoughts in mind, I have fancied that a Seabury House here in this central Oxford, with its resident priests, its own chapel where the American rite should be followed, its courses of lectures, and other aids of a social nature for the dissemination of true views of the American Church, would be of immense importance and of great use to the Church of England and ourselves in this great center of influence, Oxford.

This useful project might be commenced in a modest fashion, and, I believe, would soon attract to itself manifold gifts, the grateful offerings of friends at home and travelers abroad, happy at finding their own home in the Old Home; while it would also be a center of useful influence for the many Englishmen deeply interested in American affairs, social, commercial, political, and spiritual.

Oxford, March 11, 1891.

XXII.

I HAVE been to Keble College chapel for a Sunday evening service, and was much edified. We had a charming sermon from the Rev. Mr. Lock, one of the contributors to *Lux Mundi*. His theme was the selfishness of sin and the unselfishness of love, or the will to live selfishly, which is sin, and the will to live unselfishly, which is love. It was a sweet, tender appeal to the better impulses of the young men.

The students presented a most interesting appearance. The custom is that on Saturdays, Sundays, and Saints' Days, all shall wear surplices. As all stood in their places in that beautiful chapel, "clothed with white robes," it seemed like an act of special dedication to the service of Almighty God, a consecration of self, of youth, of talent, of power, of all the future, to high and noble purposes.

Keble College chapel is quite unlike

any other in Oxford. It is a modern presentation of the antique spirit. It glows in color from the stained glass high up on either side and at either end, from the beautiful arrangement of colored brick, variegated marble, yellow Caen stone, and dark green columns. It is one plain parallelogram of about one hundred and twenty-five feet long, thirty-five feet wide, and ninety-five feet high, divided into six bays, three of which form the nave, one the choir, and two the sanctuary. The lofty walls are arcaded and divided into panels by clustering columns, which tower up and form the interlacing vaulting of the high embowered roof. The windows are thirty feet or so from the floor, and the wall spaces beneath are filled in with pictured mosaics, or frescoes in that style. It would occupy too much space to give in detail all this imagery; suffice it to say that the entire gospel story, from creation to redemption, is depicted in the nave and choir, while over the altar is a glorious representation of our Lord, enthroned in the midst of the seven golden candlesticks.

The whole aspect of the chapel is noble, generous, and worshipful. The lamp of loving sacrifice has been aflame in its inception and construction, and it breathes the spirit of a present love, giving new form to the ancient faith.

To some tastes the place presents a certain crudeness of form and assertiveness of color, rather unpleasant. It may indeed be called shocking, but perhaps it is to provoke this very shock that the soft æstheticism of half tones and dreamy suggestions have been entirely set aside. It seems to say *anathema maranatha* to all sentimentality and haziness either about conduct or dogma, and so, the form is plain four-square, and the lines determined, and the colors pronounced.

The music to the Psalter was Gregorian, and quite well done. At times there was a slight tendency to want of true tune, a common fault where Gregorian music is sung, as it so often is, with full voice, and none of that restraint of tone, which gives such good results in Anglican chanting.

The canticles were sung to manuscript compositions especially composed for Keble College by Dr. Lloyd. Dignified in character, easy and yet interesting to sing, they would form an acquisition to our own seminaries

After the services a number of the students remained to listen to the organ voluntary at the close. This gave us the opportunity to take in the whole interior from another point of view. It is indeed a splendid structure, having a grand spaciousness about it, truly dignified, perfectly simple in its severe plan, but made graceful and beautiful by the high vaulted roof, the pictured walls, the brilliant windows, and the well-placed altar, properly furnished.

The warden of Keble received us in the most gracious manner, inviting us to tea in his beautiful house. While I sat there my mind turned back to another room, as stately, if not as spacious — the noble study of dear DeKoven, resplendent with its books, its pictures, and his own gracious presence. One cannot but admire the courage of faith, which endeavored to reproduce on American soil, the great institutions which here have place, backed up by centuries of splendid ad-

vance, rich with accumulated endow-
ments, showing on every hand, peace,
plenty, and magnificence. Dear Racine,
Vigeat Radix.

My morning was spent at St. Barnabas', at the High Celebration. I looked
with longing eyes at the long lines of
school children marshalled to their places
in church for this service. I passed them
on my way to church and watched them
as they entered. In they came with perfect order, quietly and reverently, and
when in their places, at a given signal,
all knelt for private prayer. It was beautiful to hear these little people sing Merbecke's service, the *Kyrie*, the *Credo*, and
the *Sanctus*, as well as other parts also,
in which they joined heartily. All over
the church the sound of congregational
praise was heard, and the devotion of
the people was truly Catholic and inspiring. Father Maturin was preacher,
but a rigid rule which restricts the sermon to twenty minutes, I imagine rather
restrained the free flow of his genius.
The whole service which included five
hymns was over in one hour and a quarter. Hence of course no one dreamed

of retiring before the close of the worship.

A night sermon was announced at Cowley Iron church to begin at quarter to nine, by Father Maturin. Thither we went through the moonlight, lingering among the effective bits which came in our way as we passed along. We paused by the Bodleian, with the Camera and St. Mary's before us; and then lounged over the balustrade of Magdalen bridge, watching the lights on the river, and the deep shadows of the trees. The Lecture over, but, with its John-Baptist-like refrain ringing in our hearts, we walked back once more through the moonlit streets. Magdalen Tower and the spire of St. Mary's seemed like spirits of the past; a thin haze melted their upper outlines into viewless air. They did not seem creations merely of stone and mortar, but spiritual presences, ready to speak to us of all that they had seen, if we could be alone with them, and capable of hearing with our mortal ears, their wondrous story. On we passed through the dark shadows, and broad moonlit spaces to our rest.

Oxford, March 13, 1892.

XXIII.

LET me give you a few little sketches of another day in Oxford. Come with me then, first to a breakfast with an illustrious name in the University. The hour is quarter to nine. We are received most graciously in that sweet, modest way which seems a part of the splendid training of those great souls. They know so much, it makes them humble and gentle. Soon our little group is made complete, and we take our places in the spacious, quiet room, with its pictures of departed worthies looking down upon us, and its lovely outlook upon "a garden enclosed," which, as Bacon says, is a true refreshment of the spirit.

Pleasantly and profitably for both body and soul, the hour passes. There are flashes of genial criticism upon men and books, upon great events, upon coming questions. The best side of every one comes out; wit provokes wit, and thought enkindles thought. There are, too, remembrances of the past. Pusey, Newman, Keble, Mozley, Williams — of each there is some touch of life, some anecdote which makes them live again. There is no break or stop until the time comes to say adieu, and duty calls our host to other fields, while I am left to wander forth to further pleasures.

This comes in an afternoon excursion to a spot coeval with Augustine. My friend and I take train for some miles out from Oxford, and then tramp on for miles to our destination. The way is over well-kept roads, on and on, by village churches into which we enter for a moment's rest and prayer, and then to foot again and onward. Sharp and keen the air is, but birds are singing in the trees and hedge rows, and high in air the lark utters his impassioned notes, which stop our steps as we watch the little speck he makes against the sky, and note his sudden downward flutter to the earth. " Is that the lark? " my friend asks; " it is the first time I have heard it;" to which I say, " Its song was the joy of my childhood."

At last a turn of the road brings us

within sight of our destination. A gray
tower, a long line of abbey roof, a cluster
of red-tiled cottages, groups of stately
trees, and distant hills, make up the picture. Soon we are beneath the church's
roof, but before this, we enter the vicarage, where we are warmly welcomed by
a friend who knows us both. It is the
welcome of an American to Americans.
We are at once at home. The American
flag hangs over a portrait of Washington
in the drawing room. Inserted in the
picture is an autograph letter. On the
mantel piece are portraits of Bishop Seabury and Bishop White; around are indications of love perennial for the home
across the water, dear to us all.

At last we enter the grand old church,
venerable in its Norman dignity, interesting in the evidence of transition, change,
and renewal, not the least of which is its
present condition of thorough life. Each
day the Eucharist is celebrated, Matins
are said, and Evensong rendered in choral
fashion. I cannot give detail of architecture, but can tell of the long drawn nave,
the chancel with the dignified altar and
full complement of ornaments, of the sev-

eral altars, each properly furnished, the old effigies in battered stone, priests in vestments and knights in armor, all in the light of the evening sun.

We wait for Evensong at six o'clock, which is sung by a choir of students from a missionary college close by; among them are two negroes from Central Africa. The office is most reverently conducted, and the music used was Gregorian. It was comforting to hear the low pitch of confession, Paternoster, and Creed, thus enabling the congregation to join in with ease and heartiness. The cold melodies of the ancient modes seemed exactly suitable to that simple but august spot.

After service we visited the missionary college, and took away with us the pleasant memory of the sweetest-faced young priest we ever saw, whose work lies there as instructor—his blessed work, far from the madding crowd, and great with possibilities for the onward progress of the Church of God.

In these quiet spots we get a glimpse of that real power in apparent obscurity, which has its place in many such a condition.

Once again we return to the vicarage
for more social chat until the coming of
our carriage to take us back to the railway station for Oxford.   Quickly the
time passed in that pleasant interchange of
mutual acquaintances which travellers love
to make with friends thus met.   In that
pleasant converse we learned incidentally
that a most striking religious novel we read
a year before, was written by a priest who
lived, in the hamlet, the life of a recluse.
It hardly seemed possible, but so it was.
We learned further, too, that a gentle, deli-
cate-looking cleric, to whom we had been
introduced, wielded a pen of power and
brilliancy, and that from this secluded
spot went forth reviews and articles commanding the profoundest attention and
respect.

So our day came to a close with our
drive in a welcome closed-up carriage, under a moonlit sky, to our railway station,
and so home.

Oxford, March 16, 1892.

XXIV.

MY days in Oxford drew all too rapidly to a close.   Each was opened with the daily Celebration at St. Barnabas, or some other place, then there was the morning's work of reading, letter writing, or an occasional lecture, and then the afternoon ramble, ending up with Evensong at the Cathedral, Magdalen or New.

Among my treats was a charming lecture from Sir John Stainer, on " Canonic Form," with vocal illustrations, given in the Sheldonian Theatre.   The choir was made up of ladies and undergraduates, who sang *con amore* the bits of early Italian Masses and other music used to set forth the master's lecture.

I felt it a sort of special privilege to see and hear Stainer. His music for choir use seems to hit the happy combination of scholarly form, average difficulty and melodic interest, so necessary to come

within the power, ambition, and scope of
the ordinary choir. I felt it also a sort of
duty to go and introduce myself to him
after his lecture, and tell him that his
music and himself were old friends, and
that I was glad to see him and take him
by the hand. He was standing on the
stage above me as I spoke; the unconscious attitude which he at once assumed,
crouching down upon one knee, so as to
be face to face with me, was at once an
illustration of his enthusiasm and his kind
unaffectedness.

From the Sheldonian Theatre it was
but a step to the Bodleian library. What
a grand, queer old place it is! You
shudder at the thought of such treasures
in a tinder-box of wooden floors and dry-
as-dust shelving, hundreds of years sea-
soning for a blaze, but you are reassured
when you see a placard announcing that
no artificial light or heat is ever permitted
there, and that the direst vengeance is
invoked upon any indiscreet person using
the same for any purpose whatever. A
great library impresses one like the Catacombs, and it seems sacrilegious to do
more than reverently look thereon, and

then in one's littleness pass on, leaving the occupants, bones or books, to their sacred rest, or to the potent touch, which can make them live. So from a distance we looked at the readers and librarians and passed on. We took note, however, of one or two show things, placed outside the charmed precincts of the inner bowels of the library, for the delectation of visitors like ourselves. Our eyes glanced over manuscripts and treasures of early printing from many years and many lands, but on one relic we lingered with peculiar interest. It was an unrolled fragment of papyrus on which was written a portion of the Iliad. It was taken from the tomb of an Egyptian lady in the Fayoum; and there, by the living page of Homer, lay a tress of the braided hair of her who read the words before me; and yet beyond was the skull which sheltered the human brain, and gave orbit to the eyes which saw and the mind which knew. It seemed a wrong thing to have that head there, but perhaps we deem that when people have been such an unconscionable time dead, they have forfeited their further privileges to respect

and reverence. Mummies generally seem
to have a bad time of it. I see that skull
still, so fair and round, and the braided
tress and the page of Homer.

I walked on through the great corridors of the upper hall, filled with curios,
books, and the pictures of famous men
and women; a little gift of Archbishop
Laud attracted me. It was an Arabian
astrolabe to take the position of the stars;
another near it, arranged for the latitude
of Morocco, was the gift of Selden. They
brought up visions of "curious arts," of
horoscopes and astrologers, and those who
know the heavenly bodies. I asked myself, if sun spots affect our weather, why
may not planets affect the subtler essences
of our being? All things inhere in substance, and why may not substance act on
substance through the vast mystery of the
universe?

At last, Saturday, the nineteenth of
March, came, and I had to get me to London to preach at the Savoy on Sunday, so
the afternoon saw me regretfully in the
train, sweeping away from that brave
concourse of spires, and domes, and flood-
encircled groves, which make up Oxford.

What must this last sweet glimpse be to
those who know they never will return—
"the spires and towers of Oxford, from
the railway!" But before I leave, I must
say that among the many pleasant memories of Oxford, few stand out with more
vividness than those of my little visits to
the college common rooms. There is a
delightful seclusion in them, and a cheerful companionship which is most inspiring.

You have dined in Hall and enjoyed
every moment of it—the genial hospitality, the good fare, the free open talk; but
after all those good things, something better yet awaits you; you are ushered into
the sacred privacy of the common room,
and there an hour, or more is spent in
genial leisure, wise and playful talk, and,
with it all, the inner man is by no means
forgotten.

In one pleasant room, dark with its
panelled sides and ceiling, before its ample
fire-place were ranged in semi-circle a line
of chairs and tables, all facing towards the
altar of friendship, the blazing hearth.

Surely such a custom of friendly and
scholarly intercourse must have an excel-

lent influence upon the lives of all. One
here learns how men may differ as to
view, but be the best of friends, how they
may be intent in the little circle of their
own pursuits, but yet know also, full well,
of that greater circle of human sympathies
and immortal aims which embraces all
souls within its limits. Such intercourse
must refine, broaden and enlarge those
who are within its genial power.

I should like to see such a common
room for the Professors in our seminaries,
where they could have daily social intercourse, and, for a brief hour, at least, be
removed from carking care, and the intense consciousness of the individual burden.

Another room, which will dwell in my
mind, was large and handsome. The
wax tapers upon the well-polished mahogany did not dispel the friendly gloom
of the dark corners, nor bring into prominence the features of the portraits upon
the walls. Glimpses of the past they
seemed, and not without a living sympathy with the geniality of the hour. What
a picture it all made—the leaping lights
of the great coal fire, the grave gowned

figures, sitting or standing, the table itself
a picture, and the silent servitors, ever
moving with soft tread, and meeting readily every want.

Happy hospitality of dear Oxford, this
much, at least, we may say of it, drawing
aside for a moment the veil, and letting
out between its antique folds the evidences of friendship and good feeling, ever
perennial among noble souls.

London, March 19, 1892.

XXV.

AFTER leaving Oxford, I was induced to add a few days to my last Sunday in London, by the announcement of some choice music to be performed in the succeeding week. Beethoven's Posthumous Quartette was to be produced, with Joachim as violinist, at the Monday popular concerts, in St. James' Hall. Bach's great Mass in B minor was to be given at the same place, by the Bach Choir, on Tuesday evening, and the new Requiem Mass, by Dvorak, would be performed under the leadership of Barnaby, with choir and orchestra of one thousand persons, at the Royal Albert Hall, on Wednesday night. Was I not on a vacation? Ought I not to embrace the opportunity? I concluded to do so, and, with this intent, stayed in London.

My Sunday had again its beginning at the Abbey at eight in the morning, then at half-past eleven, to the Royal Chapel of

the Savoy, where Canon Curteis received
me most cordially, and where again I renewed my acquaintance with the choir,
arrayed in their purple cassocks, girt with
crimson cords, and surplices ever flying
open down the front, making due display
of the royal colors.

The services in this quaint place were
severely simple. The choir sang, in unison, single chants to the *Venite* and
Psalter, double chants to the canticles; the
Celebration was without either choir or
music, but with great dignity and solemnity. The chapel has the organ at the
west end, on the main floor; this, with the
simple chanting of the choir, induced and
aided the good congregational singing.

My afternoon was spent at St. Nicholas Cole Abbey, one of Wren's old city
churches, on Queen Victoria Street. I
saw that Mozart's Requiem was to be
sung there at quarter past three. I found
the place well filled on my arrival, but the
quick eye of Canon Shuttleworth, the
energetic incumbent, soon espied me, and
at once I had a choice seat in the rector's pew in front. I could look around
ere the performance began, and note

every spot filled with city people, clerks, shop women, workmen, all intent on the music, and reverent in their quiet demeanor.

The choir was composed of men and women, and a few instrumentalists were in the organ loft at the west end. When the clergy entered with surplices on, the congregation arose, a short prayer was said, with the Lord's Prayer, then after the short rap of the baton, the music proceeded without break to the end. Canon Shuttleworth conducted with vigor and ability, arrayed in his surplice and Oxford hood. The music was quite fairly done, wonderfully well considering the place and the material. The orchestral players were from the East London Music Halls, and it is pathetic to know that they absolutely refuse pay for their services on those Sunday afternoons in church; they are glad, they say, to help on, and to play in such music, which they never could use otherwise. At the close of the Requiem, which was printed in Latin and English for the use of the people, the whole congregation joined in the hymn, " O God, our help in ages past,"

to the grand " Old St. Ann's " tune.   It
was glorious.   I fancied that as the choir
sat and listened, they must have felt, as I
did, that that simple strain outweighed in
magnificence all the music that went before.   It was nobly sung by lusty English throats.

The performance over, I had a little
chat with the incumbent, who told me
that when he took the church, there were
scarcely six people in attendance; now it
is well attended and crowded on special
occasions.   " Come," said he, " and I will
show you our club.   It is for men and
women, and the only one of its kind in
London."   After a climb of some steep
stairs, we found ourselves on the third
and fourth floors of a warehouse, nicely
fitted up for social purposes, and well
filled with people.   The large drawing
room looked a cozy place to lounge in,
its large and irregular shape divided off
by screens into sociable-looking nooks.
In the shadow of one sat a good-looking
young woman intent on her book, at ease
in her chair before a good fire.   At the
end of the room was a raised stage, with

scenery and footlights for dramatic performances.

Upstairs further we went and peeped into the smoking room, blue with the fragrant weed. Thence we went to the supper room, where a crowd of "pale clerks" and their lady friends were having a lay out of tea and cake. We happened in just at the moment when the "omnipotent British penny," in the shape of "thruppence apiece," was being collected from each.

What new phases of Church work and life it all sets forth. From shops and warehouses, utterly isolated in their Sunday seclusion, those lone atoms of humanity are garnered in and given a cheery word and some social pleasures. The rector moved among them a genial friend, a helper in this, their organized work to help and cheer each other.

Of the good, kind hospitality which came to me in the parson's own home hard by, a cozy nest in the very heart of this London, I can but speak. A glimpse of domestic life, of beautiful children and well-ordered home, is always a thing of joy to the traveler.

As I was on music bent, I gave up the
evening to an excursion to the northeast
of London, where I had heard that the responses and Gregorian Psalms were wonderfully given in a Dominican Priory.   I
was not disappointed and found the place
in good time, and the music to be all that
it was represented.   The monks' voices,
the choir men, and the chorister boys, entirely without accompaniment, produced
marvellous effects.   I could not make out
the service very well; possibly it had
Dominican   peculiarities.   The   Psalms
were sung antiphonally, one side in unison, the other in harmonies, with   the
treble voices taking beautiful Faux Bour-
bon parts.   The side which took the unison part always stood up while the other
side remained seated, and so alternately
from side to side through the Psalms.
Responses and Amens were all given in
this free manner without organ.   Some
of the antiphons, as sung by the Fathers,
sounded quite like the efforts of Wagner.
I did not see a soul about me pretending
even to follow the service, either with
book or posture; only at the Benediction

after sermon was there a show of congregational interest.

I came home on trams and omnibuses, through a very torrent of human life whose vortex seemed to be reached at Charing Cross.

My next night, when Joachim performed, was a joy to be remembered. I must however hasten on from this to an account of the great work by Bach, the B Minor Mass, given by the Bach Choir, which I heard the next evening. The Bach Choir itself is worth seeing. It is composed of real lovers of music which taxes the intellect, the physical powers, and then the heart. It is a sort of music which gives not up its charms to careless wooers. The members did not look like this sort of people; they were serious, refined, genteel and reverent. It was pleasant to note their pleasant greetings of each other as they straggled into their places before the concert began.

A certain tone of sadness was cast over the performance by little printed slips with mourning edge, placed upon the seats, informing the audience that the Dead March in Saul would be played as an opening piece, in memory of the composer, Mr. Goring Thomas, who a few days before had, in a fit of mental aberration, cast himself headlong to death under the wheels of a locomotive.

The work of Bach shows the tread of a giant, the tenderness of a true soul, and the heart of a faithful believer. The *Kyrie* was a great burst of confident pleadings for a known pardon and peace; the *Gloria in Excelsis* seemed the very joy of the heavens, and the *Credo*, in its every iteration of text, first gave elaboration to the faith there uttered, and then to the musical thought. I never heard so rapturous a setting in my life, and never expect to hear it excelled; so on it went through *Sanctus*, *Benedictus*, and *Agnus*, to the grand triumphant close of *Dona nobis pacem.*

With the effrontery which gray hairs can give, I boldly shared my score with a dear English girl near me; I never saw her before, and may not ever again. We enjoyed every bar of the music, and, when the *Benedictus* was ended, she said to me with a very rapture of delight: " The Hosanna comes again!" We were com-

pletely *en rapport* in the study of that
great music, and when she rose to leave
with her party, and bent her gracious
head and thanked me for the pleasure I
had given her, I felt as if we had known
each other for years. It is indeed delightful to touch the chords of sympathy in
kindred hearts, though utterly unknown
to each other in the lower planes of ordinary life. This occurs so often in one's
travels in railroad cars, by the wayside, or
in galleries of art.

On my way once to Oxford, I had a
most delightful hour with two utter
strangers. Our talk touched on all sorts
of things, from Greek sculpture to eco-
nomic questions of the present day. They
were both Oxford men, and one of them
hailed me heartily one day on the Wood-
stock Road, weeks afterwards, as an old
friend.

But touching Bach's Mass, I must add
one word more about the conductor, Dr.
Villiers-Stanford. He quite charmed me
with his gentle, quiet ways, and the genuine enthusiasm, always well restrained,
with which he conducted. There were
no frantic grimaces, no pantomime illus-

trations or suggestions for orchestra or chorus, but a grave, gentle dignity throughout all. Dr. Villiers is a handsome, tall fellow, with his years yet young upon him. I could not but admire him as he glowed with pleasure while the stupendous work unfolded itself beneath his hand and before his eyes, when choir and orchestra gave splendid utterance to the great thoughts of Bach.

I noticed that the orchestra had in it some peculiar instruments, among them a long trumpet of most slender, shining build, but with a voice like a mighty angel, pure, strong and sweet. The symphonies, too, had most vocal effects, so that it really seemed as if reeds and brasses gave forth human tones. The whole performance, continuing through two hours and a half of solid work, was most magnificent. I must add one word more yet, and that is to speak of the solemn effect of the Dead March in Saul, as played before the performance. I never had heard it with orchestra, and it gave the touching composition an added charm, increased by the standing attitude of the players and the whole audience in that vast St. James' Hall, in memory of the sad death of Loring Thomas.

The next night found me in the Royal Albert Hall, to hear Dvorak's Requiem. Let me warn my friends to be always on good time at that place. The spaces are so vast to get to your seat, that it almost seems a century before you reach it, especially if the performance has already begun, as it had in my case. But what one loses in one way is gained in another. Those who were there in time could not have my experience of that vast hall as it burst upon my sight from the almost dizzy height where I had chosen my seat. I could look down on the great concourse of people, and the ordered ranks of the enormous choir. The ladies of the chorus were all dressed in white, one side having blue sashes from shoulder to waist; the other, red sashes in the same manner. This great mass of white touched with color, and enclosed by the great background of the men in evening dress, all against the silver gray organ pipes, made quite a solemn and stately picture. It suggested to me a kind of Egyptian magnificence. The statuesque, severe drapery of the singers carried out the effect. I could not see Barnaby distinctly, across the immense space, but was glad to see him even in this dim way. He handled the tremendous difficulties of the Requiem in a wonderful manner. That vast choir did its work splendidly; but I felt sure that our own Auditorium with the Apollo Club, and Tomlins, could produce it as well. The work itself is built upon a wailing theme of four notes, which sighs out its prayer in the first phrase, and then ever reiterates it, *Dona eis requiem.* The most noble effects are the reminiscences or reproductions of ancient Church song, recurring in solemn phrase. The text is illustrated throughout by the sound, and the orchestra is used as a vast tone pencil to fill in the background with lurid colors and awful forms. Verdi's Requiem I have heard, and Mozart's, the first the more dramatic, the second perhaps the more strictly melodic; but Dvorak's has a glowing magnificence all its own, suggesting the tremendous spaces of some vast cathedral, with kneeling multitudes and responsive choirs and priestly voices uttering ever in solemn tones: *Requiem in eternam.*

Next morning I left London for a quiet visit with a dear friend, of which you will shortly hear.

London, March 25, 1892.

XXVI.

I HAVE had such a charming visit
of five days at B—— B——, including therein a lovely Sunday, that I
must give you, as far as possible, the ben-
efit of it all. Away then by train to the
station, where a neat trap and smart liv-
ery await us, and off we go through
wooded scenes to our destination. We
pass village after village, each with its
cross-tipped church, until at last the noble
tower and spire of B—— B—— sa-
lutes us. We are received at the hospitable parsonage, and are soon at our ease
before a fire in our bedroom, dressing for
dinner. That pleasant meal, begun at
half-past seven o'clock, is enjoyed in a
large old hall, hung about with good pictures, and decorated with all manner of
bric-a-brac. We are a small company,
the young parson and myself *tête-à-tête*.
There is much to talk about, our first
meeting years ago, our accidental coming

together, years after, in New York, our
common friends, our common antipathies,
our likes and dislikes, our hopes, our experiences, our failures, our resolves.

Dinner over, we pass the rest of the
evening in the spacious drawing-room,
whose walls glow with artistic treasures.
There hung a genuine Raphael, there a
Giotto, there a Perugino, there a Mem-
ling, old Florentine pictures with back-
grounds of gold, flanked by Flemish
tryptychs and quaint panels, while beneath were rare old cabinets laden with
curious glass and old china. Books too
were in abundance, but the best thing
there, to my mind, was the modest young
owner of it all, heir to all this wealth, and
of a noble line, earnest and enthusiastic in
his work as a village parson. As an in-
dication of that genuine love which comes
into the heart of the true priest, I must
tell you of a picture on his library man-
tel-piece. It was a photo of a London
policeman, a fair, good face of a stalwart
steady man. "That," said my host, as
he saw me looking at it, " is a picture of
one of my young fellows, a dear good
lad, now one of the picked men on duty

on the Strand. He writes to me every
fortnight." It warmed my heart to think
of the two correspondents, the London
policeman and his young rector in the
country.

Next morning I was at the handsome
church for the daily Matins. Dainty and
magnificent both, was the beautiful structure. The tower, spire, and nave date from
the thirteenth century and are in perfect
preservation. The choir and chancel have
been erected within the past few years,
joining on with absolute harmony to the
more ancient part. All has been put in
the best order by Bodley, the great English church architect. The church, though
small, had a most noble effect, from the
spacious windows in north and south
aisles, in the choir, and in the clere-story.
Mere verbal description of architectural
detail seldom conveys a clear idea. Stand
then in the nave and look at the choir
end; you see a perfect rood screen, with
the rood upon it and St. Mary and St.
John; over the altar is a rich gilt reredos
with a quaint old German picture of the
Ascension. On each side are rich hangings, above a glorious window of perfect

glass, while the altar has its proper ornaments, and standard candelabras in addition. The nave and choir are lit with
candles held in chandeliers and candlesticks of beaten iron, made in the village,
thoroughly artistic. Before each chorister, on the desk is a tall taper. You can
imagine then the effect of all this at night
— a flood of light among the singers and
the people, while in the high roof is
gloom, except where a line of gold or a
touch of color reflects back the lustre from
below.

The services on Sunday were a delight.
The sweet bells called us to the early Eucharist! Through the churchyard paths,
from the village near came the little groups
to the silent waiting church. It was good
to kneel in the restful quiet of such a
place and await the reverent Celebration.

At eleven, the church was filled for
choral Matins. What a rest it was to sit
in the return stalls in our surplice, and have
all done for us, and take no other part than
that of a worshipper. Our turn, however,
came afterwards, for we were put up to
preach at night, and preach we did, and I
fear too long, but the inspiration of time

and place was irresistible; we forgot that the congregation expected to get home in good time for supper, the service beginning at 6 o'clock. That long sermon was rather on our conscience, until at night we got some relief from our host's butler, as he brought us, when we were in bed, a cheering and soothing posset for our cold, accompanying the same with the assuring and flattering remark: "That was a nice sermon you gave us to-night, sir; we all liked it." I turned in to sleep at peace with all mankind.

The next day I had a drive of sixteen miles with my genial host, from one parsonage to another. A snow shower had fallen during the night, but ere noon it had vanished. The sky was pure cobalt, well furnished with sumptuous masses of fleecy clouds. Young lambs by hundreds gamboled in the pastures, a fresh green tint of new wheat was on the brown fields, and so we bowled along over good roads, by church after church, and village after village, until at last the spire of B—— B—— again came in sight and we were once more at home.

I must speak also of the village school,

with the organist school master and his assistants. Happy boys and girls in one long, picturesque room, with its good ventilation and roaring fireplaces at each end. Happy little ones in the kindergarten department, big with the importance of their momentous head work and other weighty concerns. I must speak, too, of the quaint blacksmith shop, where I recognized several of the choir men and choristers, and revelled in the artistic beauty of iron deftly wrought into sanctuary lamps, chandeliers, candlesticks, and other objects useful for home as well as church.

It was an added pleasure to my Saturday, Sunday and Monday in this sweet place, to have a big batch of American letters handed me to read, before I was out of bed this morning.

B—— B——, March 28, 1892.

XXVII.

MY stay in Brighton during Holy Week and Easter has been a sort of climax to my " Winter Vacation."

A note from the good vicar of St. Bartholomew's, the Rev. T. W. S. Collis, reached me in Oxford inviting me down to take what duty I desired, on Palm Sunday and the week following. I undertook to preach twice on Palm Sunday, twice on every day in Holy Week, except on Good Friday, when I was to conduct the service of the " Three Hours," and preach also at night. This episode of work during my vacation was most welcome.

On my way to Brighton I passed through London. It was the day of the University boat race. This I could not by any possibility attend; but as I had seen one of the crews on the river at Oxford, and had also once seen a similar

event from the vantage ground of a charming lawn, with the added interest of good
company and a good luncheon, I did not
so much miss the sights on this occasion,
when there would be nothing for me, except the jostling crowd.

London never looked brighter. It was
all aglow with light and color, and seemed
like a new place under the phenomenal
sunshine. It was pleasant to see the public interest in the boat race; dark blue and
light blue vied everywhere for prominence. It was on the cabbies' whips, on
the caps of the omnibus conductors, in
buttonhole bouquets, in the shop windows,
on ladies' hats, everywhere. I had a little
visit to make between my trains up at
Chelsea, near Cheyne Walk, sacred to
Carlyle, the Rossettis, George Eliot,
Whistler, and hosts of artists and literati.
I do not wonder at the selection of such a
place for residence, for it is a sheltered
nook well withdrawn from the crush and
roar of London, and has the Thames before it, with the double daily sweep of its
grand tidal current. Opposite, too, is
Battersea Park; I was tempted by its trees
and shrubbery to take a stroll there my-

self before making my call. It was delightful to find such a spot so accessible in crowded London. Great stretches of green sward were there, flocks of sheep on the grass, and embowering branches to shut out all else but a dream of sylvan seclusion. I enjoyed it all, especially the little groups of children, happy and contented in their sports.

My little visit was upon a dear good lady, whom I had not met for twenty years, but seeing that I was in England, she sent for me to talk of her son in Holy Orders in the American Church.

It was pleasant to see the mother's heart evince its love, and to read the newspaper clippings which told of the young civil engineer going out to Indiana, how he took interest in Church work as a layman, how he attracted the notice of his priest, how he was introduced to the Bishop, how he entered Gambier, and in due time took holy orders, and was in a few months to be made himself a priest. Our pleasant talk had to end, for I had to get back into the Strand before I took my train for Brighton. The tide was at the full, the river was thick with returning steamers and boats from the races, a bright sparkle was over everything, and it seemed the very thing to do, to take a steamer down to Charing Cross Wharf. Over and over again I had seen it all, but it seemed fresh as ever as we went from station to station, reaching at last the superb group of the Parliament Houses and Westminster Abbey.

The ebb and flow of the Thames make it seem majestic, to have a life and force all its own; it is like the throb of being or the conscious action of a mighty will. The Thames at London is really noble; above tidal effects it seems merely a pretty stream, but it is that, charming in its ever peaceful course through quiet greenery.

I must say that I never tire of the grand effect of St. Paul's as seen from the river. It towers up with graceful, majestic simplicity, above the life of London. On this bright day it seemed more glorious than ever. The flowing lines of the dome reaching up to the great cross, suggested the confidence and harmony of the Faith, soaring above the varied and contradictory aims of time. Underneath was the turmoil of housetops, apparently a heap without ruling plan, but each the centre of keen personal aims. Above was that shapely dome surmounted by the cross, telling of the one great plan of God, for the salvation of the whole world.

Landing at Charing Cross Wharf, I took a farewell turn or two once more in that ceaseless tide which ever pours through the Strand, and then a penny bus to Victoria station, and off to Brighton. The way was cheered by a charming group in the railway carriage, a young couple with child and nursemaid off for a holiday. Why did I not speak to them and have a chat! He was so bright looking, with a dark complexion, clear eyes, well cut features and kindly air. She was also beautiful and a brunette, with a great dash of yellow in her hat that became her immensely. The boy was a fairy, lovely as a dream, clad in sailor fashion, with a Neapolitan cap, and was half the way, deep in a picture book. The maid was by no means a beauty, and occupied her time with *The Graphic* and *Tid Bits*. In one corner of the car was another passenger, a young lady plainly dressed, deep in the perusal of a reporter's note book;

one of that numerous class, "self-support-
ing women." I watched her intent air,
her business look, her occupied manner,
and thought of the toil and suffering such
gentle souls endure, and hoped she had
her reward. We all, close together, yet
far apart, whirled on to Brighton on a fast
train, through the green English fields
dotted with cricketers, foot ball players,
and all the other signs of that healthy out-
door British life.

At last we pulled up at the station,
when the young lady reporter asked the
gentleman opposite if this was the place
to get out at. "Really," said he, "I do
not know, but fancy it is." It appeared,
after all, that I was the only person in the
compartment who had been to Brighton
before. It was many, many years ago,
when I went to call on a dear friend of
DeKoven's; strange that his name and his
fame should come up before me again
here in Brighton in this visit, for a few
days after my arrival, when invited to
have my picture taken at Fry's, the emi-
nent photographer's, the young man in
attendance asked me if I knew Dr. De-
Koven. "Years ago, sir, I saw him in

Bath; I was then a very young man, but I was wonderfully taken with him."

A hearty welcome awaited me at St. Bartholomew's vicarage, and soon I was settled with study and bed room, as contented and happy as if I had been there for years. The vicar suggested ere it should grow dark, a visit to the church. We entered that vast interior, and the awful Cistercian simplicity of it was overpowering. It is all plain brick, but even as a vast host made up of mortal men has its own sublimity, so this great pile told its own story, in its own grand way. The light streamed in from the upper windows in a great flood, softened by the evening hour. The effect of the interior of this great building is superb. There is a flood of light, but you see no windows. They are concealed from view by the immense thickness of the walls, and the supporting buttresses which project into the church. In its way, it is quite as impressive as Westminster Abbey, and for purposes of worship excels it.

The great altar with the seven lamps hanging in front dominated the whole building. It stands elevated fourteen steps from the main floor, and is, with the great baldachino, most noble in its proportions. This church is one of the seven built in Brighton by the Rev. Mr. Wagner, who is still living. They must have cost a million dollars at least, for this one, St. Bartholomew's, cost one hundred thousand. Oh! but what a church for grandeur and simple dignity it is! I had the extreme pleasure of being introduced to the Rev. Mr. Wagner. Quiet, unaffected as a child, his bright face lit up with a holy light as I told him how St. Bartholomew's impressed me. " I suppose," said he, " you must have some great churches in your wonderful Chicago?" A whirl went through my mind of all the trials and perplexities, and efforts, necessary in our difficult sphere to effect anything; and so, with a gasp, I said we had some churches that were quite creditable and witnesses to much love and sacrifice, but none, said I, as yet, like St. Bartholomew's.

Next Sunday was Palm Sunday. We had the blessing of the palms and their distribution, with a procession, before the High Celebration. It was a tremendous sight to look out over that vast congregation, their faces touched by the vivid light of the bright day, and above them the clouds of incense, through which the sun's beams grandly gleamed in four great luminous slanting bars, from the four lancet windows in the end of the church.

The music used was the *Missa Regia* with Merbecke's Creed, evidently well known, as the people joined in heartily. The sermon was my share of the work. It was the first time that I had preached to such a congregation in England, but a feeling of encouraging sympathy came up to me from the vast mass of upturned faces quietly and intently awaiting my first utterance. Before the High Celebration began, I had been into the " little church," an adjoining building, crowded with children, boys and girls, while a *Missa Cantata* was in progress; at this, the little ones, with their own choir, and with full ritual propriety, say the entire service. The young priest who officiated was especially happy in his sermon and catechizing, and the children bright in their answers. A force of teachers and sisters were stationed with the children, and the best order and reverence prevailed.

The usual number of guilds, for all classes, men, women and children, have place in this parish, with a club also for men, but the busy work of Holy Week prevented my attendance or study of them.

Of all that week I cannot speak, as I was a great part of it myself. It was a blessed week for me as, day by day, I looked out over the attentive and sympathetic congregation. The " Three Hours " service impressed me most. There must have been at least a thousand people present. The singing was inspiring. My theme was, " Life Lessons from the Seven Words," and, as hymn after hymn rolled out with its familiar words and well known tune, I was comforted and delighted.

The church was a very *De profundis* in itself, every ornament gone, the altar in black, and back of it on high, an enormous Tau cross in oak, with the place for the sacred Feet, the nail holes in the wood, and above all the Title with its inscriptions in Hebrew, in Greek and in Latin. During Matins and the Reproaches which preceded the Three Hours, I could not keep my eyes from it. That empty cross, with a great white cloth draped over the extend-

ed arms, seemed to me the most solemn
memento of the Crucifixion I ever saw.
It preached silence and sorrow over all
that vast church and hushed congregation.
The " Three Hours " moved on as I have
ever found, with a strange rapidity.   Intense occupation takes away from time the
quality of extension.   A moment may be
seemingly infinite, and hours as a mere
hand-breadth.

On Easter Even I spent hours in the
church watching the busy workers getting
ready for Easter.   Flowers were everywhere, tufts of the dear yellow English
primrose, spirea, lilies, snow-white aza-
leas, and other blossoms I did not know.
Above the great altar was the sexton plac-
ing the enormous candles and flower vases,
afterward to get the finishing touches
from the sisters and their helpers.   Of
this sexton I must speak.   He is a wiry
little Japanese, with coal black hair and
grizzled beard, keen and alive all over.
Fudi seems never idle; the whole of the
vast church he cleans himself, and con-
stantly as it is thronged, it always seemed
dustless and ready.   He seemed to look
at me as a sort of fellow foreigner, for he

was always most pronounced with his hearty salutation, bringing the open palms of his hand front face to his forehead whenever we met, with a bright smile of recognition. It is a picture to see him ring the bell from his place at the end of the church. He has a loop for his foot, and with that leverage he makes light work of it. When he rang the bell three and thirty tolls at the close of the Three Hours service, beginning at a signal from my uplifted hand at the stroke of three, I could not help thanking God that Christian Fudi was there to join in the work.

While I was loitering about the church one of the wardens met me and told me that he had been in connection with St. Bartholomew's over twenty years, and that for years he was the only man in attendance. What a contrast from to-day ! — a distinctive characteristic of the services is now the large attendance of men. It struck me at once as I went round with the procession on Palm Sunday, and the impression remained with me during all the services of Holy Week, especially the solemn service of the Three Hours.

It was my happy privilege to celebrate

at six o'clock on Easter Sunday; that was
the second service of the day, and four
more were to follow before the high service at eleven. I need not say how one's
heart remembers distant friends, and the
souls of those so well beloved who have
gone before, on such an occasion. The
very separation of time, and space, and
condition, seems a spiritual connection
rather than a real barrier. The soul can
leap out over all that divides, and triumphs
over them thus in its inherent wonderful
power. At this service there was a goodly
number to receive, and glad I was to see
the seamed and blackened hands — the
hands of labor — held up for the Bread of
Life. How touching to look at them,
some of them those of mere children. One
little lad had a C. B. S. medal hung by a
red cord about his neck. What a solace
it is to administer at the altar, and to note
the varying conditions of men, and to
know that He can satisfy every need, and
cleanse from all defilement.

At the nine o'clock Celebration I was
in church again to assist at the Communion, and after that, at the High Celebra-

tion at eleven. This was preceded by a
solemn procession most impressive. Baden Powell's "Hail! Festal Day," was
grandly sung, the ever recurring chorus
being heartily taken up by the vast congregation. In this as well as in various
portions of the service, most efficient aid
was given by a skilful cornetist. With
rare tact he accompanied all through the
music, now on the euphonium, now on the
trombone, the French horn or the cornet.
The man's heart was in his work. I
knew why afterwards, when I saw him
come faithfully to serve at some of the
early Celebrations on week days.

The music of the service was *Eyre*
in E flat. Its familiar cadences carried my
thoughts far away. It was grandly sung.
The whole solemn service with priest,
deacon, and sub-deacon properly vested,
and with most careful and dignified ritual,
was an object lesson in the reality of the
historic Church, the dogmatic verities of
historic truth, and the solemn importance
of religion.

Father Maturin was the preacher.
His sermon was a brief but intensely im-

passioned oration on the necessity of keep-
ing a due proportion between the heart
and head in matters of the Faith.   The
Magdalene at the empty tomb declaring
with a rush of feeling that her Lord was
taken away, was the type of love regardless of reason, while Thomas who would
not believe unless he could put his fingers
into the print of the nails, and thrust his
hand into the wound in the side, was a
type of reason regardless of love.   The
thought was enlarged upon with a master's hand.   It was a glorious sermon.

In the afternoon I attended the children's serivce and catechising.   There
were no flowers, no sentiment, no Easter
eggs, but there was positive dogma and
clear teaching, and Catholic worship.   The
whole vast church was filled with children.
It was beautiful to see the little ones watch
the banners as they moved by in their
mysterious and grave motion.   To me
there was something impressive in the
gentle and unimpassioned faces looking
down upon us from their silken folds.
My own thoughts were reflected from
the rapt faces of the little ones, as they
watched their banners carried past.

At Evensong the church was more than crowded. Father Maturin again preached. A grand procession brought the services of the day to a splendid close.

Brighton, April 18, 1892.

XXVIII.

MY last day in England had peculiar charms and was full to the brim with interest. The friends with whom I was staying in Bolton, Lancashire, asked me what I would like to see, the Town Hall, the Museum, the Picture Gallery? They said nothing of the mills, nor the wild moors all beyond, breezy, and grandly monotonous, so I replied that I could see town halls and museums almost anywhere, but that I should like to go into a cotton mill, and then, afterward, take a tramp over the moors, while I had the opportunity.

Down from the little villa, mercifully hemmed in by shrubbery from the great chimneys, we descended to one of the enormous cotton mills. I was taken through the whole process, from the raw cotton to the delicate and completed cocoon-looking bobbin, ready to be transformed into the woven fabric. Machines were stopped for me, the interior intricacies of their wonderful construction were moved slowly so that I might observe their complicated and beautifully certain operations. It was all like a kind of magic; there was a thunderous din, and silent figures moving about among the whirling spindles, dreadfully intent upon their unceasing toil. Conversation there could be none, and the ceaseless whirl of the wheels forbade idle loitering. As I walked about from room to room, in the heated air, laden with cotton fluff, and saw the silent, busy figures intent upon their work, I understood as never before what a luxury the loud talk, and the coarse frolic, and the free movement of a holiday, must be to such work-people. What a relief, too, must be the song and the chat when day is done, and silence settles down upon the mill; but here I am wrong, silence scarcely ever settles on the mill. It is worked by two sets of hands, and runs continuously, day in and day out, except during the hours from 2 A. M. until 6 A. M. On, and on, and on, the vast machinery must ever go. It is too delicate, too complicated, too ponderous, to be ever allowed to get cool.

The operatives had a sort of fascination for me, as they went on so ploddingly and yet keenly alive to their toil. In one room were two girls feeding a roaring machine with lumps of raw cotton which, with a graceful motion, they tore apart and flung in special order upon a moving frame before them. The noise was terrific. Their eyes were intent upon their work, as their arms, with incessant motion, fed the voracious machine.

This was the first process from the cotton bale. We followed on until the cotton wool, like cobwebs upon dewy grass, was drawn from the carding machines, on and on until the perfect thread was formed, and spun upon the great machines, each with its thousand spindles and hundred feet of length.

Keenly the master operative with his boy assistants watched those thousand threads. Backwards and forwards from either side, the great machines advanced and receded, while in the ever-changing space between, the workers were in constant motion, stepping mechanically over

the advancing wheels, never making a
false step; eye and hand and thought ever
alert and at work.

The atmosphere was hot and moist, to
suit the tender filaments of the cotton
wool; the floor looked dark and polished,
saturated with oil; on this, with bare feet
and grimy, scanty overalls, moved the
spinner, his piecers, and the boys. I
watched them intently, 'mid the fearful
clatter of the wheels, the constant motion
of the machinery, and the silent alertness
of their own ceaseless toil. It enlarges
one's heart and increases one's sympathies to see such sights.

From the mills to the moors was a
transition, and a grateful one. A carriage drive brought us through outlying
suburbs to our destination, where, send-
ing our vehicle on to meet us beyond, we
tramped across the breezy heath, over
moss and fell, another way. The free air
of heaven never seemed so good before.
In the dim distance, on every side, were
the tall chimneys of collieries and facto-
ries, a forest of human energy and toil.
Smoke in clouds hung ever them, but
above our heads the larks were singing,

the bright clouds floated by in billowy
state, and the bee and blossom were at
our feet.

We all too soon reached our carriage
and found a neighboring old English inn
not a bad place to rest a little, where we
duly enjoyed the wine of the country in
the shape of beer, and bread, and cheese.
The room in which we sat was worth
seeing. It was wainscoted and seated
with comfortable benches, almost as dignified as a cathedral choir. On the man-
tel-piece was a picture of Archer, the
jockey, surrounded by numerous lesser
lights in his exciting profession, and the
room was further ornamented with several brilliant hunting scenes. The imagination could easily fill in a winter's evening with "cakes and ale," and songs of
hound and hunting horn, and "jolly good
fellows, every one."

From the moors back to town again,
and then by train for Chester, which I
duly reached by 6:10 P. M. Here were
other dear friends to welcome me, friends
linked by kindred memories of those long
at rest. When I announced that I was
to take the Irish mail that night for

Kingstown, *via* Holyhead, there was much disappointment, but with true delicacy the most was made of my brief stay. Out then, after tea, for one more walk about the walls of Chester. What a lovely close to my day, beginning in the morning, at the mill; at noon, upon the wild moors; at evening, at the Minster, drinking in the beauty of the setting sun, as it shone upon the Dee side, and the towers and battlements of Chester! It was a lovely walk, looking down upon the green sward of the great race course, dotted with cricketers, and boys at sport; out over the graceful stretch of landscape to the Welsh mountains; on by the waters of the Dee, watching the changing lights, and the fishermen at their work; on and on, until we reached the cathedral, and leaned over the parapet of the old walls, chatting of old times and watching the darkness creep down over all, until the lace-like forms on gable and pinnacle were alone distinguishable in the dark and sombre mass. It was all most beautiful. We strolled back in the darkness to the home fireside, where, in pleasant converse, we passed the time until the midnight hour, which took us off, through Wales, by Holyhead, across the Irish Sea, landing us in the morning at the picturesque harbor of Kingstown.

Our last day in England, with its pictures of the mills, the moors, and the Minster, will not soon be forgotten.

Adamstown, Ireland, April 22, 1892.

XXIX.

MY stay on the return to Ireland, waiting for the steamer, which I take to-morrow at Queenstown, has been of the quietest description. As I passed through Dublin, I learned that the Synod of the Church of Ireland was to convene in a day or two, at Christ Church cathedral. There was a momentary desire to stay over and witness it, but sunshine and clouds and green fields and utter rusticity for eight or ten days before embarking, seemed altogether better and more inviting, and that was my choice. I had in my retreat, it is true, the echoes of the world I had left; pleasant letters from Brighton, invitations to come again and enjoy English hospitality, farewell letters from dear friends. I had, too, my American mail, and with all these I was happy; with the dun cows grazing before me, and lambs at play by their mothers

in the grass, days were never dull with
such companions.

The walk by the trout stream was
always beautiful; the rapids, the shallows,
the deep pools, the wayward curves, the
water plants, the flying birds, the possible
fish and fishing, the lovely landscape, the
great bulk of the distant mountains — it
was all good.

I took the steamer " Brittanic," of the
White Star line, from Queenstown, on
the afternoon of the 5th of May. While
waiting for the arrival of the mails from
Dublin by rail, many of the returning
Americans came on shore, availing themselves of the opportunity to visit Irish
soil, making merry parties on flying jaunt-
ing cars, laden down with golden blossom of the gorse, fragrant lilac bloom,
and great bunches of purple rhododen-
dron.

The luxuriant foliage and genial shelter of Queenstown never seemed more
beautiful. The hours of waiting soon
were past, the mails were quickly handled,
and we were steaming along, once more,
the rock-bound coast, out into the great
deep.

On the morning of the 13th my voyage was over, and once more I was on American soil. It was indeed lovely to come on deck in the early morning and find the steamer at anchor off Sandy Hook. The Fort, with its green velvet grassy embrasures, the trees in full foliage, and the ever-welcome stone spire of Névesink church, made a pleasant picture to look upon after the grand monotony of the sea.

The voyage, however, was not, for me, monotonous. It was a long holiday. In the early morning there was a glorious plunge in high proof, genuine salt water, then black coffee, a little rest, and a good brisk walk on deck, and *then* breakfast, with a good sea appetite. The hours never wearied. If I wanted utter loneliness, I could get out on the forward turtle back, and have before me the great circle of the sea, westward, and not a soul in sight. The huge steamer seemed to carry myself alone. If I wanted memories of the past, I could get back in equal solitude at the stern, and fancy the British Isles, where I spent so many pleasant months, beyond the waves which bounded my

gaze to the eastward. If I wanted company, I also had that. My opposites at
the dinner-table were two most interesting
men from Pittsburgh, who had been out
in Roumania to prospect for petroleum.
They were of Scotch-Irish extraction, the
third generation from the old home, full
of fun, vigor and American breeziness.
Their Roumanian experiences were worth
listening to. By my side was a good
stout friend from gastronomic Baltimore.
Beyond was a saturnine young English-
man, from a Florida orange grove, gen-
tlemanly and good-natured under a most
alligator-like severity. Nor were other
interests lacking. One could excite to
gentle conversation the fair mummies on
the deck, swathed in shawls and enthroned in their steamer chairs; or the
smoking-room was at hand, where the
incense of friendship was ever ablaze; or
the steerage could be looked into, with all
its nationalities and various types of humanity. As for reading or writing, that
was out of the question; a cerebral excitement comes from life on the sea, which
at once arouses to action and prevents any
positive concentration. It provides the

best possible excuse for doing nothing.
In this happy condition were most of the
occupants of the smoking-room, aroused
only from their delicious Havana by the
announcement of the day's run, or the
necessary replenishment of the sustaining
pipe or goblet.

Our saloon passenger list was somewhat limited, about seventy in all, but
among them I again found evidences of
the smallness of the world. The first day
out I made acquaintance with a fine
young fellow who had been to Liverpool
with a load of cattle from the West. I
found him to be one of De Koven's boys
at Racine, a graduate at Yale, a Churchman and a gentleman. How much we
had to talk of in our many walks on deck!

Two splendid fellows I found also,
Chicago men, buyers for one of our
mammoth houses, on their return trip
from Europe. Another, in the same line,
I found from New York, who knew one
of my old choristers at the cathedral, now
grown up and a yearly buyer in Paisley
and Manchester.

A charming young lady I found to be
the niece of a brother priest—my class-

mate in the seminary, and a dear friend ever since. An English lady bound for Wisconsin, I found to be on her way thither to join her brother, whom I knew well.

A well-to-do, elderly gentleman from New York, who had just done the holy places in Palestine, and also Egypt and the Nile, I found to be the parishioner of a dear friend of many years' standing. So when Sunday came about, I felt that we were a lot of friends together, and the service and sermon was a labor of love.

The voyage all through was most pleasant. For a day or two the sea was "deeply, darkly, beautifully blue," but after that it took on a soberer tone. We had no storms, but we had the great long roll of the Atlantic, which told of tumults further off. Of these we heard when we got on shore, for an incoming steamer, travelling at the same time, was badly damaged by mountainous waves, whose rhythmic echoes alone, we experienced.

There are few sights more glorious than New York harbor, from the city to the sea or from the sea to the city. One greets it ever with fresh enthusiasm. In majestic order the great ship, with its attendant tugs, slowly gains the wharf; gently as a child going to sleep the huge bulk moves on; surely, like fate, the moment of landing comes, and for the thousand souls on board a new life begins. Some step out to pleasant friends and hearty greetings — such was my happy lot — others to begin again the battle of life in a new and untried land, among utter strangers.

I looked with deep interest at the large stream of steerage passengers, over nine hundred, filing off across the dock to the tenders which were to convey them to the Bureau of Immigration; and then at my fellow passengers in the saloon, all intent upon the ordeal of the customs. There were courteous farewells among us, and many hopes of renewed meeting, and soon, in due time, I reached again the hospitality of 1 East 29th st., which had been wafted to me across the broad Atlantic, and cheered me up through all the way.

As I rang the bell at the well-known door, I turned about and took in once more the bright flowers, the splashing fountain, the merry sparrows, with Belteshazzar and Chedarlaomer in feline majesty looking lazily on. I was aroused from my momentary reverie by the voice of the good doctor, who had himself, unperceived, opened the door behind me, greeting me at the same time in cheery tone, with the classic welcome, " *salve*."

May 13, 1892.

XXX.

WHEN one gets home from foreign parts, familiar sights and sounds take on a strange peculiarity, which they never seemed to have before. How queerly free and easy the average New York policeman looks, compared with his London brother. What a lounging aspect at the cab stand. How odd the cosmopolitan names which follow each other on the shop signs. How independent and inconvenient the indiscriminate use of sidewalks for all sorts of business purposes. How tired and eager looking the average man. How mature and self-possessed the children, how bright and wide-awake the whole aspect of things, how confident of self, how heedless of rubbish and disorder, amid splendor and magnificence on every hand.

Assertive architecture, bright skies, gay colors, drive, dash and bustle everywhere and, through it all, a certain inde-

pendent carelessness which shows itself in
the faces of all about you. This is New
York. I saw more than this though on
on my first day back. The chestnut trees
were in full bloom at the Worth Monument, and the great stretch of Madison
Square was a bower of greenery. There
is no street scene in my mind that has
more of glitter in it than that spot in New
York, where Broadway runs diagonally
across Fifth avenue at 23d st. I stood
there a short time to watch the crowd
which never passes by, but is always passing. It is a steady stream of American
life which nowhere else presents such
contrasts of all sorts and conditions
of men and women, the vast majority
showing evidence of that levelling-up
process, which is the great distinctive
aspect of American city life as compared with all others. The shop girl
trips along dressed a-la-mode and the
mechanic or clerk gives little evidence
of any special calling. A certain touch
of fancy and vivacity is in all about
you. It is on the shop fronts, on the
street vehicles, on everything. This dash
and *elan* appears in the very services of

the Church. The clergy do not look as if their surplices were thrown on, their stoles are straight and neat. If hoods are worn, they have a fastidious exactness of cut and color quite remarkable. I saw four on in one vestry, all different and attractive. A touch of American improvement is given to every object, including even the Church itself. I strolled into Grace church and had a look round at that representative building, and noticed the peculiar comfortable luxuriousness which one never sees in churches abroad. I also noticed that the choir, which formerly had stalls at each side of the chancel, was moved back to the gallery over the west front. It seemed to be a very sensible proceeding. A choir of professional men and women, close up to the altar at each side, is not always sure of being a help to devotion at all times. If also they sing elaborate music, needing a conductor's hand, which certainly they ought, the mechanism of the musical process becomes disagreeably prominent. Other churches will follow this lead and, possibly, we will see ere long a revival of west gallery choirs. I am sure there are

few more distressing experiences than the
cluttered up vestry rooms of little churches, where priests and choir vest together,
and the horror is continued and intensified
in small chancels where choristers, organ,
organist, bellows-blower, priest and altar,
are all huddled together in a space sometimes less than twelve feet by ten!   Better choir stalls well down in the nave
among the people, with the organ above
at the west end, or, just as well, the choir
surpliced in the west gallery.

The indiscriminate use of choirs of
men and boys illy trained and bundled into
our small chancels, is not an American
improvement, although too prevalent a
use.   The echoes of English choirs are
yet in my ears, which one hears from the
distance of nave or transept, or stands
beside in the spacious choir, while on beyond is the altar, withdrawn within its
own sacred space   We have much to
learn and much to get rid of in our surpliced choirs, and perhaps must bring the
well-trained adult voices of men and women once more to lead the music of many
of our churches, from the quiet vantage
ground of the Western Gallery.

During my few days in New York I made a visit to the site of the new Cathedral of St. John the Divine and tried to imagine what a grand place it will be when completed. The position is magnificence itself. It is a crowning point of the great upheaval which rises on the western side of Manhattan Island. It will tower up and be a landmark from the lower bay. It will dominate the Hudson river. It will crown the verdure of Central Park with its soaring splendors. It will say to millions through all time, " This is none other than the house of God and the very gate of Heaven."

All this in the future; but at present, even, it is very beautiful. The old Leake and Watts orphan asylum, now no longer used as such, occupies the grounds. An old-fashioned pillared portico accents the front; above is a great cross. Ample stretches of greensward are on every side, and grand trees and flowering shrubs suggest the palace of the sleeping beauty. The kiss must be a golden one which will waken all to life, but the coming chink of that is already heard. On the gateway was this inscription, which gives a significant hint of the spiritual life which gold cannot buy, "for the price of wisdom is above rubies." Here it is:

CATHEDRAL
OF
ST. JOHN THE DIVINE,
TEMPORARY CHAPEL.
HOLY COMMUNION
EVERY SUNDAY
AT 9 A. M.
ALL ARE WELCOME.

As I looked at that sign my mind reverted to a scene I witnessed over thirty years ago, when Bishop Whitehouse held the first services in his cathedral chapel at Chicago, which he afterward enlarged and named the Cathedral of Saints Peter and Paul. As I looked at the prospective magnificence before me in New York, I felt that the western fact made the eastern hope a splendid possibility. But my mind went back farther yet to the first public utterance of the second Bishop of Illinois, when in his address of either 1851 or 1852, he outlined the Cathedral system, declaring it to be a necessary adjunct to the Episcopate, being, as he afterwards formulated it, "the complement of the headship."

I would like to see in the Cathedral of St. John the Divine, New York, a grand recumbent monument to Bishop White-house with this inscription thereon: "The founder of the first American cathedral."

During my stay in New York I also visited the new St. Agnes'. It presents a most imposing appearance from the out-side, making, with its rectory, parish build-ing, and chapel, a magnificent pile. It is in the new and growing part of the west side of the city, at 92d street and Tenth avenue. The residences here are detached like those on our best Chicago boulevards, and the streets are ended by the distant greenness of Hoboken seen across the Hudson river. The House of God seems, as it ought, to be the best house there. From the outside at least, you feel satis-fied that the $800,000 which all cost was well spent. Frankly I cannot say as much for the inside. The first shock was to see the view on entering cut off by an overhanging gallery at the west entrance. The second was to feel the incongruous and strange mixture of pointed arches un-der the great central tower, with rounded arches farther on, and on every hand in the rest of the structure. The third was to find that the lantern of the tower, which should flood the inside with soft, radiant light from above, was all blocked up with darkest stained glass, with a glint here and there of ruby or of yellow. What should have been a fountain of purest light, was an impenetrable cavern, a place of gloom.

The sugary profusion of light marbles and gilt mosaic gives a luxurious air to the whole edifice. The redeeming feature was a certain archaic effect, produced by the marble altars and stalls and other furniture, suggestive of early Christian art, as seen in San Clemente and the catacombs.

I sat down in the pews and watched the people coming in to rent their sittings. We must, of course, have pewed churches, but my mind reverted with thankfulness to St. Augustine's and St. Chrysostom's both free, and to dear old Trinity at the head of Wall st., and I thought with gladness of how nearly that also was a free church, and how much it was ahead of anything like the new St. Agnes'. I thought, too, of graceful Trinity chapel.

Yes, also of classical St. John's, doomed, alas! to destruction, and felt that we may have gorgeous experiments in architecture, but few such truthful exponents of real art as the churches I have named. To say that the Parthenon has not been surpassed need not seem a slur upon present achievement. It simply states a fact.

I also happened into the new Zion and St. Timothy awkward name, but really beautiful church. It is one of Halsey Wood's designs, and has the notes of that peculiar stateliness which so eminently pertains to his structures. It is, inside and outside, brick, and, except for a little pew upholstery, has that honest, sturdy severity of the best English work. The sexton told me with great unction how well they were off, having a good endowment, free pews, and an overflowing congregation as liberal as one could wish. Like everything else in America, a free church must come under the general rule of success, or it will not succeed. It must have a good start, a large edifice, and every evidence of life and prosperity, and then the people will flock in.

This St. George's, Stuyvesant Square

has, an endowed rectorship, yielding
$10,000 per annum, a fine grand church,
inherited from pew-renting days, and old
families of wealth and prominence hooked
on to the old place by ties of years and
blood.

I was at St. Zion's — no, Zion and St.
Timothy's — at an evening service on
Sunday, and enjoyed the great congregation and the fine singing of the people.
The sermon, by a bishop who has an empire for a diocese, was over an hour and
a half long. How differently things appear to a clergyman when he is a worshipper among the people. The sermon
was not too long for me; the amazed look
of the young men and others near me, as
period after period rolled off, was a useful
and telling study.

Before starting back again to the West,
I made one more visit to the General
Theological Seminary. "How," said I
to myself, "will it all appear after the
majesty and extent of Oxford?"

Well, it holds its own remarkably
well; I may add even, that I have not
been into a college chapel service in
Oxford which, for heartiness and spon-

taneous beauty, could touch the chapel of
the Good Shepherd at the Seminary in
New York. The rolling tone of the
Gregorian Psalter was splendid, the *personnel* of the students most attractive, the
air of religious feeling most apparent, the
entire absence of officialism and petrified
routine most pleasant; and the building
itself, too, was not lacking in the presence
of the " exceedingly magnifical."

The comely altar and reredos of costly
marbles and alabaster, the well-finished
pavements, the solid and tasteful fittings,
the resonant organ, the harmonious and
intelligently arranged stained glass, produced a whole, which made an honored
kinship to Magdalene, to Exeter, to Keble, and to New.

If we should ever get so un-American
as to put a great wall all round Chelsea
Square, the entrance to such an enclosure
and what is or will be there, would be
like a vision of some of Oxford's good
things. But as it is, the seminary is a
" thing of beauty." May it be " a joy
forever."

Two other incidents in my stay East
have fastened themselves in my memory.

One, my first Celebration after returning, at the Midnight Mission; the other, a visit to St. Peter's, Morristown, New Jersey, where I found a beautiful church just completed except the tower, which brought back to life here in this western land the best type of sacred building one could find in the old home, untouched by glare or finical ornament, but grave, solemn, real, precious, beautiful, chaste, a very symbol of the Living Church, a noble bride adorned for the heavenly bridegroom.

New York, May 18, 1892.

XXXI.

ONCE again on a train for the West, the voyage over, friends in New York revisited, and sweet old memories renewed, we start on the home stretch for Chicago!

There is a feeling of splendid achievement in the *personnel* of a limited train on one of our great railroads. When I say *personnel*, I do not mean merely the officers or their assistants, but the very train itself, including in that term the whole equipment.

To walk through from end to end, from dining car to the library and smoking-car, is a revelation of energy and intellect combining to make travel a delight.

You have crossed the ocean on a vast monster whose food is fire and whose breath is steam. Under the scales of this leviathan you have slept in peace, and in its bosom you have been cherished with royal dainties: and now, a tamed monster of like

breed, a flying dragon of strange verte-
brate variety, bends its back to your foot
and whirls you in luxurious safety across
the continent.

It gives one a renewed home enthusiasm to dash on so splendidly, up the
glorious valley of the Hudson, and on and
on to the great level stretches which await
the traveller by the mighty lakes.

The Hudson river never seemed more
lovely, nor the Catskills more grand. Silently one watched the flying panorama,
vainly longing to possess as a permanent
pleasure the framed-in landscape of even
one car window.

The first long, splendid dash brought
us to Albany, where one fain would stop
and refresh himself with the beauty of
the first structure in America which fitly
expresses the cathedral idea. There, at
least, one can find a grand building, well
conceived, the work well-done, and all
beginnings harmonious — foundations for
nobly designed further progress. Nothing
to undo, and much yet to accomplish in
faith and love.

While we were taking a step or two
on the platform in the brief stoppage at

Albany, Bishop Coxe passed by and took our train for Buffalo. He looked well and returned our salutation with all the grace and courtesy which are so eminently his. I wish I could tell all the nice things he said, and the compliments which made it evident that at least on the score of personal health my " Winter Vacation" had been to me a success.

The day wore on through New York State. A sweet oblivion fell over all the night of our journey, and my waking outlook was nearing home, but yet in Indiana.

After the varied outlines of English scenery, the majestic monotony of the sea, the splendors of New York and the glory of the Catskills, the first look on a western landscape has a sort of spectral lightness.

The few simple elements of scattered trees, flat horizon, and vast aerial spaces, all help to produce this effect. The sky was palest blue, with a stiff array of formal fleecy clouds stretched in lines across it, while beneath were the branching trees just touched with vivid green, and the earth, yet bare of summer bravery, stretching out in its vast indefiniteness, telling us that we are in "the West."

Another voice with a like message soon sounded out to us from the right hand. Ere long we were by the mighty lake. A strip of yellow sand alone separated us from the dancing waves. The vast bend of the great circling horizon, tremendous as the ocean, uttered to us again the thrilling message: "This is the West."

Nearing the very end of a long journey has in it a certain thrilling interest of unrest and expectancy. Months have fled, changes have come, much has happened, the past has gone; the future to come, what will it be?

The pleasant friends of the long railroad journey have already said adieu, the baggage man is in the train; on we fly through the far-reaching miles of Chicago, until at last we roll into the station and alight to the pleasant greetings of faithful friends, and then, off through the whirl of Chicago to our welcome home.

While the strange new light is yet on all that surrounds us here, let us jot down our returning experience. We note with

interest the vast array of primordial cells
of social life in the long stretch of artisan
cottages which reach out for miles on the
prairies. The great school houses loom
up, cross-tipped spires are not altogether
wanting, but the denominating feature of
all is "business, business, business." The
clanging bells of the constant trains ring
" business, business." The huge eleva-
tors roar out "business;" the vast piles of
stately warehouses, splendid in architecture and Egyptian-like in their solid
grandeur, utter in deep tones, " business."
The sky-scrapers that dwarf Cologne or
York Minster, shriek " business." The
unmerciful cable cars, the Juggernauts of
commerce, snarl out " business;" the toss-
ing crowds are intent on " business."
Huge gaps are seen here and there where
vast buildings have been torn down by
" business," to make room for greater
" business." It looks as if a tornado had
struck the whole place and left piles of
building material on all sides scattered
about, but the cyclone whirl which has
done it all is merely the breath of " business."

Amid all this din of " business " a note

struck in of strange, antique tone. It was in accord with much that I had observed in England where religion has been cared for in the past and fortified for the future. It witnessed to the reproduction here in Chicago of that system by which a "rent charge" is made to support the services of religion. This strange tone in the midst of all Chicago's din of business came from some mission buildings close by the railroad tracks, over which I was passing. There I saw a magnificent plant consisting of chapel, mission rooms (medical and social), manual training schools and gymnasium, all surrounded by block after block of flats, the rental of which sustained the entire fabric, paying all expenses of the mission, giving at the same time healthful, tasteful and inviting homes to the people, and affording them also, absolutely free, a place of worship and the humanizing influences of religion and pastoral care. Here, on what is designated a non-sectarian basis, a common-sense Chicago millionaire has adopted the Church's old plan of securing religious privileges for the masses, by a rent charge on occupied property.

This business man represents the State giving privilege of occupancy to its citizens, under the condition that they shall pay a rent charge for the support of religion within their boundaries. The old revives amid the new.

It is pleasant to see all this amid the whirl of " business." Vast structures have been run up during my six months' absence. I am almost a stranger in what were once to me familiar streets. Now all is changed or changing. I visit the World's Fair Buildings, and am tired out by the mere walk from each to each; and all around. Through ornamental gardens, and by lagoons, an army of workmen are hard at it, and all branches seem to move on together. Here, a crowd of men arrayed in India rubber clothing are planting a variety of aquatic plants in the ornamental waters; there, electricians; beyond, engineers; aloft, machine fitters joining the enormous arches of the great Machinery Hall; on every side work, work, while the great lake lies fast asleep beyond, and the great city stretches out its vast depths on either side. But the time will come, yes, is coming, when there will be the fair fruits of this "business." The Newberry Library looks noble and inspiring in its rising beauty in Washington Square. The Chicago University already begins to present a splendid appearance. The foundations of the new Art Building are in, upon the Lake Front; Kretschman's inspired Columbus will also soon be there in breathing bronze; and so, little by little, or rather I should say, much by much, Chicago emerges from the youthful ravenousness of insatiate business, to the wider and calmer condition of solid acquirement, reposeful pleasure, and refined rest.

Amid all the roar and bustle of civic existence, it was sweet to note the modest but most eventful indications of Church life, the growth of six months. Among these, the new parish house for the mother church of the West, St. James', Chicago, the great organ at the Epiphany, the projected churches for St. Paul's, Kenwood, St. Paul the Apostle, Austin, and other edifices, close to, or in the city; but beyond all this, the spirit of work and progress which characterized the diocesan convention, where

so many of my brethren gladly welcomed me back among them from England after my most pleasant, profitable,
and happily ended " Winter Vacation."

Chicago, May 31, 1892.

www.ingramcontent.com/pod-product-compliance
Lightning Source LLC
Chambersburg PA
CBHW030103030726
47498CB00007B/2236